Rio Grande Stories

Carolyn Meyer

Harcourt, Inc.

Orlando   Austin   New York   San Diego   Toronto   London www.HarcourtBooks.com

First Harcourt paperback edition 2007
First Gulliver Books edition 1994

The Library of Congress has cataloged a previous edition as follows:
Rio Grande stories/Carolyn Meyer.
p. cm.
Summary: While preparing a book which highlights the people
and traditions of the diverse culture found in Albuquerque,
a group of seventh-graders discover interesting things
about their city and families.
1. New Mexico—Juvenile fiction. [I. New Mexico—Fiction.]
I. Meyer, Carolyn.
PZ7.R4815 1994
[Fic]—dc20 93-33639
ISBN 978-0-15-200548-1
ISBN 978-0-15-200066-0 pb

Text set in Granjon
Designed by Trina Stahl

C E G H F D B

Printed in the United States of America

For Ernesto Antonio

WELCOME TO
RIO GRANDE MIDDLE SCHOOL

There are two things you should know about this unusual school.

First, the school, the class, the students, and their teachers and parents are purely fictional. The young people from Native American, Hispanic, African American, and Anglo cultures exist only on these pages and in my imagination. All the events described in *Rio Grande Stories* are my invention.

Second, since their original publication these connected stories have inspired *real* students in *real* schools all over the United States to talk with family, friends, and neighbors and to write their own stories and put together their own books, each as uniquely different as the communities in which they live.

Though the stories in this book are fiction, the places I've written about—the cities, towns, and pueblos of New Mexico—are as real as the Rio Grande itself. The Big River is the shining thread that stitches together histories and cultures both ancient and modern, from the Native Americans who were here from the beginning, to the Spanish conquerors, explorers, and settlers, and the later Anglo arrivals who came—some peacefully, some not—and stayed.

I am one of those late arrivals. Having lived all my life on the East Coast, I had never been to the Southwest before I drove to Taos in the spring of 1978 for a two-month stay at a writers' colony. I decided then and there that New Mexico would be my home.

In some ways the stories of the young people in *Rio Grande Stories* reflect my own. I struggled to enjoy eating fiery chile. I took Spanish lessons. I set out luminaries at Christmastime and sang hymns in Spanish as "Mary" and "Joseph" made their journey from house to house. Eventually I settled in Albuquerque and married into a family with deep roots in Nuevo Mexico. I listened to their stories about Padre Martínez, about the "hidden Jews," about the first black explorer, about the Navajo code talkers. My mother-in-law taught me how to make *bizcochitos*. I put down my own roots.

Then life took an unexpected turn, and we moved to another part of the Southwest—the high plains of Texas—traveling to New Mexico as often as possible. After five years we moved back to Albuquerque, but during that homesick period away, I conceived the idea for *Rio Grande Stories*. I'm home now—for good, I hope—and remain grateful to family and friends and to the many Rio Grande writers, poets, historians, and artists of all cultures who have given me insight into this area and its rich diversity.

—Carolyn Meyer

TABLE OF CONTENTS

Table of Contents

Table of Contents

JEREMY STEINBERG

✖

The Heritage Project

JEREMY STEINBERG printed this in block letters on the first page of his new notebook and decorated it with flourishes:

Heritage Project
Seventh Grade
Rio Grande Middle School
Albuquerque
Bernalillo County
New Mexico
United States of America
Northern Hemisphere
Planet Earth
Solar System
Milky Way Galaxy
Universe.

At first Jeremy had not been at all pleased about taking a city bus clear across town every day to attend Rio Grande Middle School. Most of his friends were going to Jefferson this year. But after only two weeks of school he was beginning to change his mind.

It had been his mother's idea. When she heard that the old R. G. School, a stark brick building with tall, old-fashioned windows, had been remodeled and was being turned into a progressive magnet school for talented kids, with special new programs like this Heritage Project, she couldn't wait to sign him up.

"Think of the opportunity, Jeremy!" she said. "It could be a wonderful experience for you. You'd get to meet all kinds of different people and learn about their traditions, their cultures. Diversity and academic excellence— you can't beat that."

"Yeah," said Jeremy, still unconvinced. He wished he could get all that and be with his friends, too.

His father teased his mother about camping out on the school lawn in her sleeping bag so she'd be first in line to register Jeremy. It turned out not to be such a joke: she waited for hours, but she got him in.

So here he was, and Jeremy had to admit, he kind of liked it. As his mother predicted, there were lots of kids in his seventh-grade class who, like him, were "magnetically attracted" (his father's phrase) from all over the city, as well as other kids who had grown up in this neighborhood near the river and had been at this school the year before. A small group of them had been accepted into the Heritage Project, a combination of history, geography, social studies, and language arts that counted as three classes. The idea was to develop individual study projects that showed how each student's family history fit into the history of the United States. Mr. Wilder, the teacher in charge of the program, seemed like a pretty reasonable guy. Jeremy thought he'd probably look better when his beard, just starting to grow and still ragged as an unmowed lawn, got a little thicker.

Not everyone at R. G. got into the Heritage Project. You had to be interviewed by Mr. Wilder and to demonstrate awareness and interest in your family's history and culture. Jeremy told Mr. Wilder about his great-grandfather, who had come from Russia a long time ago and made his living as a peddler, and about the peddler's son, who opened a shoe store in Albuquerque and built it into a successful chain. The shoe man, Jeremy's grandfather, had four daughters but no sons. After he died, three of the daughters took over the shoe business, but one, Leah, wanted to be a social worker. Leah was the last one in the family to marry, and her sisters teased her about being an old maid. But then she met Albert Steinberg, a social worker from New Jersey who had waited a long time to find a wife, and they got married. Jeremy was their only child.

"My parents were pretty old when they had me," Jeremy told Mr. Wilder. "I don't have any brothers or sisters." He didn't tell Mr. Wilder that he was sometimes embarrassed because his parents both had gray hair and were always the oldest parents to show up at any school function. People often mistook them for his grandparents.

But he was pretty lucky, Jeremy explained. His other grandfather, his father's father, had moved out from New Jersey to a retirement home in Albuquerque after Grammy Steinberg died five years earlier. A tall, stooped man with only a fringe of white hair circling his bald, freckled head, Gramp Steinberg seemed ancient to Jeremy. He leaned heavily on his cane. But there was nothing old about Gramp's mind. "Eighty-four years old and he remembers everything," Jeremy's father marveled. "His brain's in better shape than mine." Not everyone had such an interesting grandfather.

Every Friday on his way home from work, Jeremy's father picked up Gramp at the retirement home and brought him to their house for the Sabbath meal. Gramp invariably insisted on a report from Jeremy on his doings.

"The Hebrew lessons?" That was always his first question. "You're studying hard?"

"Sure," Jeremy said, which was stretching the truth a little. He was preparing for his bar mitzvah in the spring, but he didn't particularly enjoy those Hebrew lessons.

"Good! Good for you!" Sometimes Gramp would quiz Jeremy, asking him to recite the names of the months in Hebrew or to repeat a particular prayer. Jeremy was always relieved when this part was over.

"And school? What about that?" he'd ask, his bright eyes fixed on Jeremy.

"It's fine, too, Gramp." And these days that *was* the truth.

"Well, tell me something about it. I'm interested, you know."

So Jeremy had told him about the Heritage Project. And now there was this new thing: the fund-raising project.

• • •

On Monday of that week at the morning assembly in the large combination cafeteria-auditorium that they called a cafetorium, the student body was informed that everybody was going to be involved in a project to raise money. The principal, Mrs. Salazar, wanted to buy a piece of sculpture to put on the lawn next to the school sign.

"Something that will signify the unique nature of our school," she'd explained. "Something that will symbolize how the Rio Grande—both the school and the river it's named for—brings us together. Your challenge, as individual students and as students working together as a team, is to discover a creative way to contribute." Translated, that meant each group in the school was supposed to come up with a money-making scheme.

The chorus was the first to announce its project: it would sponsor a bake sale once a month. The debate club planned to put on seasonal potluck suppers. That sounded good to Jeremy—all the valley kids would show up with enchiladas and burritos and *chiles rellenos*. The computer club, to which Jeremy also belonged, decided to sell candy, which at least would be an easy sale—his dad would buy everything Jeremy took home.

Every day since the assembly, the Heritage Project kids had spent a big part of their triple class period brainstorming for a scheme to raise money. *Brainstorming* was Mr. Wilder's word for sitting around and tossing out every idea you could think of, no matter how weird and goofy, until you couldn't come up with anything else, and then eliminating the ones that were either grossly stupid or totally impractical until you got down to something you liked or at least didn't hate too much.

Mr. Wilder had scratched his scruffy beard and made a list of their ideas on the board. They came up with quite a few, from holding car washes to raising rabbits to sell. Nothing seemed exactly right. The class wanted to come up with something more relevant to what they were studying.

Then on Friday morning something one of the students said clicked in Jeremy's brain. "What if we write a book?" he burst out. "Everybody in the Heritage Project does a chapter, and we print them up and sell them. I'll bet we make more money than anybody else because everybody will want to buy a book and so will all their relatives." He was getting pretty excited by his own idea, and he looked around to check how the others were reacting.

Mr. Wilder wrote Write a Book under Sell Rabbits.

"What kind of a book?" Rosa Gonzales asked. Rosa was a tall, serious girl with gold-rimmed glasses that made her large brown eyes seem even larger.

Before Jeremy could answer, Peter Kingston, who lived in the foothills close to the Sandía Mountains, said he wanted to write a horror story, something with vampires and gallons of blood. At that Mr. Wilder held up his hand and said, "Maybe we'd better figure out what this book is supposed to be about first."

Back to brainstorming. It was slow in the beginning, but as the class got warmed up, the ideas started coming faster and faster. All the stories, they decided, ought to have something to do with life in New Mexico, past and present. The stories could be part of the students' individual study projects, but that wasn't a requirement. "Just so it's *interesting,*" Jeremy said.

Rosa Gonzales came up with "Tortilla History." Then April Ellis, a blond girl with freckles, volunteered to write "Chile—Red or Green?" because, she explained, she'd had so much trouble getting used to spicy hot chile when her family moved from California. The kids convinced Pauline Romero to write an article about Indian pottery because she had come to the city from a pueblo famous for its pots.

"Our people aren't from around here," Franklyn Cox told the class. "My sister and I were born in Virginia. We got transferred from Florida. We lived all over. My dad's in the Air Force."

"You could research the history of African Americans in New Mexico," suggested Rosa. "My dad's always reading history, and he told me there've been some important ones."

Mr. Wilder, who had been jotting notes all along, beamed at the class. "Looks like you've got the start of a good project here," he said. "Now you have to figure out how to get it done."

"I'll be the editor," Jeremy announced.

"I've already thought of a title. We'll call it *Rio Grande Stories,* for the school and also for the river."

"Yeah, good idea, Jer!" a couple of kids said.

But Rosa Gonzales, who had said she'd write about tortillas, shot Jeremy a freezing glance. "Are we supposed to volunteer to be in charge?" she asked. "Or are we electing people? Because *I* want to be editor. Since there are two of us who nominated ourselves, we have to have a democratic election." She sat down, arms folded across her chest— smugly, Jeremy thought.

The kids gaped. Mr. Wilder chuckled. "I think she has a point, Jeremy. Are there any other volunteers? Or nominations for the job of editor?"

There were none.

"Let's debate," Jeremy said, feeling sure he had the best qualifications. The book had been his idea in the first place, and he had suggested the title. Besides, they could use the desktop publishing program on his father's computer. But when Rosa told the group how passionately she felt about writing and language, Jeremy could sense the other students leaning in her direction.

In the end the students elected Jeremy Steinberg managing editor and Rosa Gonzales literary editor. Jeremy was satisfied with that, and Rosa stopped looking smug and smiled broadly. Everybody applauded to show their support, and Jeremy and Rosa were excused to go to Mrs. Salazar's office to inform the principal that the Heritage Project class now had its plan to raise money for the school sculpture.

"You should write the preface, Jeremy," Rosa told him later as they hurried to the cafetorium for lunch. "I think it's important to start with an overview. Something *sweeping,* you know?"

Jeremy gritted his teeth. Rosa was what his mother called a "take-charge kind of person" and his father translated as "bossy." "Okay," Jeremy said. "I'll call it 'How Grand *Is* the Rio Grande?'" *There,* he thought, *that ought to shut her up for a while.* But he couldn't resist adding, "I'm also planning to do one of the stories. I have an idea for something very unusual."

"You do? What is it?"

"You'll have to wait and see."

Why did I say that? Jeremy asked himself as he pushed his tray through the lunch line.

Because, in fact, he didn't have the slightest clue what he would write about.

. . .

Now on Friday evening as Jeremy's family finished their Sabbath meal, Jeremy told his grandfather about *Rio Grande Stories* and how it was his idea, stopping just before his conversation with Rosa when things got sticky.

"Excellent!" Gramp said. "And what is your project for the Heritage Project project?" That was a typical Grandfather Steinberg question; he liked to play with words.

"I'm doing the preface," he explained. "And probably something else, too," he added, wondering what on earth that would be.

For the next few days, Jeremy worked on the preface. He spent time in the school library researching the facts.

The Rio Grande is 1,885 miles from its source in the Rocky Mountains of southwestern Colorado to the Gulf of Mexico, 465 miles shorter than the Mississippi. After leaving New Mexico, the Rio Grande forms the border between Texas and Mexico. In spite of its length, it is unnavigable, too shallow for boats to travel inland more than a few miles from the gulf.

He made notes on the mountains in the north and the farmlands to the south. He found out about the rainfall—there isn't much—but snow melting in the mountains accounts for most of the water in the river. He thought he'd include something about the altitude, seven thousand feet above sea level in Santa Fe. He began to get bored. This wasn't exactly "sweeping."

He was beginning to be sorry he had agreed to write about such an unexciting topic. The more the Heritage Project kids talked about their family histories, the more Jeremy fumed. Everybody else had such interesting families, it seemed to Jeremy. His was dull. Who cared about selling shoes?

And then there was the matter of his boast to Rosa that he was going to do something unusual.

The next Friday evening, after the Sabbath candles had been lighted and the prayers said and the dinner started, Gramp asked his usual questions: Hebrew lessons? Heritage Project?

"And your project for the Project project?" he asked, savoring his joke.

"Okay, I guess. I've collected a lot of facts about the area, but I'm kind of stuck for a really good story," Jeremy confessed. "Being Jewish and all," he added lamely.

"And you think the Jewish people don't have an exciting history in this part of the world? Nonsense! Of course we do," Gramp said. "In fact we have a long and fascinating history in New Mexico."

"I've told Jeremy about the traders and merchants who came out here in the nineteenth century, Pop," said Jeremy's father. "Some of them were sutlers—they supplied the army posts with provisions. Wouldn't that make an interesting topic, Jer?"

"I suppose so," he said, sighing. But it sounded impossibly dull to him, not at all what he had promised Rosa.

"I suppose you'd prefer adventure, mystery, something like that, eh, Jeremy?"

Jeremy admitted that he would.

"Well, then," Gramp said, leaning across the table, "I have just the person for you to meet. You come by and visit me on Sunday afternoon. I'm going to introduce you to a very special friend of mine. It might be a good idea for you to bring your tape recorder."

Jeremy tried to get his grandfather to tell him something about this mysterious person, but Gramp merely smiled and shook his head.

"You'll see," he said. "You'll get your story."

Sunday afternoon Jeremy's mother drove him to the retirement home. "Do you know what this is about?" Jeremy asked her.

"Frankly, I can't imagine. He wouldn't tell me, either. 'It's a gift for Jeremy,' that's all he'd say. He also made it clear that I'm to drop you off and pick you up in an hour. I learned a long time ago that if that's what Ben Steinberg wants, then that's what Ben Steinberg gets."

"A lot like Rosa Gonzales," Jeremy muttered.

His grandfather was waiting for him in the visitors' lounge. With him was a tiny woman with a cloud of wispy white hair. She sat in a wheelchair with a rainbow-colored crocheted afghan across her knees, her gnarled hands folded in her lap.

"Ah, here's my grandson now!" Gramp proclaimed, and the old woman peered up at Jeremy and smiled a crinkly smile. "This is my good friend, Mrs. Naomi Luna. And because she's my good friend, she's agreed to tell you a story. Did you bring your tape recorder?"

Jeremy nodded and showed them the palm-sized recorder his father had lent him, still wondering what this little old woman with the Spanish name could tell him about the Jews.

"Mira," the old woman said, fiddling with something on a thin gold chain around her neck. "Look."

Jeremy looked closely. It was a tiny Star of David. Quickly she dropped it back inside her blouse, where it couldn't be seen. "But why are you wearing that?" he asked.

"Because," she said so quietly he had to lean close to hear, "I am a Jew. A secret Jew. A *hidden* Jew. *Marranos,* they called us—swine. Our story goes back to the time of Columbus." She flashed a brilliant smile at Jeremy's grandfather and reached out to take Gramp's big hand in her small one. "My friend Benjamin helped me piece it all together. That's why I'm doing this for you. You may tell my story, but you must promise to keep my name a secret. My children would not approve. They deny everything."

"I don't understand," Jeremy said, bewildered.

"You will," Gramp said. "Now just turn on your tape recorder, and we'll explain it all. By the time we're finished, I promise you'll have a real Rio Grande story that will be as exciting as anything in your book."

Jeremy clicked on his recorder. Grandfather cleared his throat. "My name is Benjamin Steinberg," he said in a deep voice, "bringing you the story of"—he paused dramatically—"'The Hidden Jews of New Mexico.'"

An hour later, when the tape ran out, Jeremy shut off the recorder. Even Rosa Gonzales, he felt sure, would be impressed.

THE HIDDEN JEWS OF
NEW MEXICO

❖

Recorded by Jeremy Steinberg

BENJAMIN STEINBERG: *The story of the hidden Jews of New Mexico begins more than five hundred years ago. It is 1492—the year that King Ferdinand and Queen Isabella of Spain have sent Columbus off in search of a new route to the Indies. In this year the same Spanish king and queen give the Jews in Spain a choice: convert to Christianity or leave Spain.*

Maybe 200,000 Sephardic Jews (Sephardic *is from the Hebrew word for Spain) lived in Spain with communities in almost every city and village. You can imagine what a terrible choice they had to make! About half of them decided to stay and convert to Christianity. They were called* conversos. *But Ferdinand and Isabella suspected that many of these* conversos *were still secretly practicing Judaism. And many were! That made them heretics in the eyes of the Catholic Church. And so the king and queen established the Inquisition, whose job it was to find and punish what other Jews called* marranos, *meaning "swine."*

Remember this name: Torquemada, the Grand Inquisitor. He made sure that those who got caught were tortured and put to a horrible death—burned at the stake!

The rest of the Jews who fled from Spain settled in other countries. Some of them eventually made their way to Mexico—or New Spain, as it was called then. But eventually an Inquisition was established there, too, to hunt down marranos. *Some of those Mexican Jews pretending to be Catholics may have managed to sneak into the area that is now New Mexico, far from their tormentors in Mexico City. But their Jewish heritage was always kept a deep, deep secret.*

NAOMI, A HIDDEN JEW: *I grew up a Christian and a Catholic. All my life we went to mass every Sunday. But when I reached my early teens, my mother told me a great secret: "Somos Judíos," she said. "We are Jews." At first I didn't believe her, but she said she heard it from her father, and so on, all the way back, and it was true. My father's family, the same thing. My parents were lucky to meet each other because, as I found out, if you marry somebody who isn't from that background, it can be very lonely. Nobody knew exactly how it happened, that we were Jews. But my mother told me I must keep it a secret, it was dangerous not to, and so I did.*

Every Friday night my mother lit candles in our home. She had given me a Jewish name, Naomi. And she would never, ever serve pork, which Jews are forbidden to eat. That used to make me mad, because all the other kids were eating chicharrones, *fried pork skins, and I was never allowed to touch them. And I couldn't tell the other kids why. We learned when we were very young not to talk about what we did at home. Those were family matters, and we understood that we must keep secrets. Keeping secrets was a way of life for us. It has always been so.*

MR. STEINBERG: *The reasons for becoming a hidden Jew were obvious. But later, after the Inquisition ended, many hidden Jews continued to keep the secret. They wanted to be part of the communities in which their ancestors had settled, and everybody in those communities was Catholic. There was a great deal of prejudice against Jews, and hidden Jews didn't want to be set apart, isolated, so they pretended to be Christian. Think how hard it is to remember your ancestors' faith when it's been kept a secret all those years, all those generations!*

NAOMI: *When I married, I told my husband my secret. I didn't think it was right to keep this secret because we had promised in the marriage ceremony to forsake all others and become one flesh. I thought he would understand, but he didn't. He got very upset. "You can't be Jewish!" he yelled at me. "The Jews killed Christ!" And he told me I must never say such a thing again. So I didn't, not even to my own children. I kept the secret until he died. It was very lonely for me after my parents died, and my brothers and sisters were afraid to talk about it. It was easier to go to mass every Sunday and not think about it.*

MR. STEINBERG: *As they kept their big secret and pretended, generation after generation, most of them forgot their Jewish roots. But a few tried hard to pass along the traditions to their children. Later generations kept some of the traditions, like the Sabbath candles, the prayer shawls worn by the men, sometimes the unleavened bread baked around the time of the Jewish Passover, which coincides with the Christian Lent. But they didn't know why they did these things. They did them only because they knew it was part of a secret tradition in their family.*

NAOMI: *I talked to a rabbi, and now I'm learning about the Jewish faith of my ancestors. But I am still a Catholic, too. It's too hard to give up everything I believed for so long. And my children, my grandchildren, my great-grandchildren, they are all Christian, even though I tell them they are partly Jewish, too. My sons laugh at me and say I'm a foolish old woman with a head full of nonsense, and my daughter gets angry, just like her father did, but two of my granddaughters are curious. They want to know more about it, and they promise not to tell their parents what I tell them. "It's a secret!" I say. "A big, big secret!" So this is how it is for me: on the outside where the world can see it, I am a Catholic. On the inside, where only God can see it, I am a Jew. A Mexican-American Catholic New Mexican Jew. How about that?*

TONY MARTÍNEZ

※

The Great-Great-Great-
Great-Great-Who?

AFTER school and on Saturdays Tony Martínez hung around his father's barbershop, Joe's Haircuts While-U-Wait. His job was sweeping up after each customer stepped down from a chair, either his father's or his grandfather's. Tony liked the barbershop smells, the clicking rhythm of the scissors, the joking conversation of the men with white towels tucked around their necks.

His grandfather always snipped away in silence, but his father kept everyone entertained. Tony thought someday he'd be a barber, working with his father after his grandfather retired. Then he'd be the quiet one, the one who made sure the scissors were sharp and the customer got his hair cut exactly the way he wanted. His mother hated that idea—she wanted him to be a doctor or a lawyer, some kind of professional—but his father took it for granted they'd be partners in a few years.

"Meet my son Antonio José Martínez," Joe Martínez would say to his customers, even when Tony had already met them several times, "direct descendant of Padre Martínez of Taos." This was his father's way of bragging, not only about Tony but about himself and his own father, reminding his customers that he belonged to an important family.

Being a direct descendant of Padre Antonio José Martínez was, in this neighborhood, a little like being a direct descendant of Abraham Lincoln. Padre Martínez was a man everyone knew had been important a long time ago, back when New Mexico was still part of Mexico. On the wall opposite the mirrors, Tony's father had hung an old-fashioned portrait of Padre Martínez, a sour-looking man with his hair combed down flat on both sides of his head. *He could have used a good barber,* Tony thought, *and some cheering up.*

There was a problem in claiming to be a descendant, though, and Tony's mother,

Alicia Martínez, was always quick to point it out: Padre Martínez had been a Catholic priest, and since priests didn't marry they weren't supposed to have children. Without children, no descendants. The good padre, whom Tony's mother admired as much as everyone else, would never have done anything sinful like having children without being married, she said. More likely her husband's family was descended from one of the priest's brothers.

But Tony's father got annoyed when she reminded him of that and brushed away her arguments. "Come off it, Alicia," he'd say. "He was a man, a human being, he did what men do, and he had children. That's nothing to be ashamed of. Right, Tony?"

Tony, trapped in the middle, never knew what to say, so he always mumbled, "I don't know." What he did know was how important it was to his father that Tony agree with him.

Just a few weeks ago, before school began, Tony and his parents and three little sisters had driven up to Taos to a Martínez family reunion. It was held at the old Martínez Hacienda, the massive adobe home that Padre Martínez's own father had built for his family. All the rooms opened onto interior patios with not a single window in the thick outside walls. That was for protection from the Indians, Tony's father explained.

Hundreds of people showed up for the reunion. Most of them didn't even know each other, but they all had the same thing in common—they were related to the priest who was a hero to the people of northern New Mexico.

Tony took his sisters out to the fenced-in pasture behind the hacienda to see the burros, two big gray ones and a baby only a couple of weeks old that could make the most amazing leaps. All the kids were hanging out there, wanting to pet the little white burro with brown spots. Tony saw a boy who looked about his own age. They sized each other up before they spoke.

"What's your name?" Tony asked.

"Antonio José Martínez," the boy replied. "What's yours?"

"Antonio José Martínez."

They laughed. "There are others besides us, I bet," the second Tony said.

It was funny, but it also sort of bothered Tony that he was not the only one here. His father had always made him feel that he was unique.

"My mother doesn't like the idea that I'm descended from a priest," Tony confided to the second Tony, wondering if the other boy's mother had the same argument.

The second Tony's dark eyebrows lifted. "Who says you are?" he asked.

"My father."

"Huh." That was all the boy said, and Tony figured that meant the other Antonio José Martínez couldn't make any such claim for himself. Tony immediately felt better.

Then a bell rang, calling them back to the larger patio, where rows of chairs had been set up facing a small, raised platform. An actor dressed as a priest in a black cassock with a white collar appeared. He had slicked his hair down flat so that he resembled the portrait in the barbershop. In a one-character play, the actor showed how Padre Martínez always did good things for the people, taking their side no matter what—a lot like Abraham Lincoln.

The audience stood and applauded when the performance ended. Afterward, Tony decided to go up and try to talk to the actor. He seemed to know so much! Tony had to wait a long time for all the aunts and uncles and cousins to finish asking their questions. Finally he got his turn. "Do you think it's possible for me to be Padre Martínez's great-great—however-many-times—grandson?" Tony asked him.

"Sure it's possible," the actor said. He had put on his glasses and recombed his hair. "Some people think he might have had children. But other people don't. There's no proof one way or the other. So you can believe whatever you want to believe."

Tony felt disappointed. That settled nothing. Before he could ask anything more, he saw his mother searching for him, a worried look on her face. Tony recognized the look. His father wasn't like that—he was always smiling and jovial, unless he was mad about something, and then it was a totally different scene. Tony's mother was more even-tempered but very serious. She worried a lot. Tony wished he could be more like his father.

"We've been looking for you," she said. "It's time to go. We've got a long drive back to Albuquerque."

Alone in the backseat while his little sisters slept in the rear of the station wagon, Tony listened to a familiar argument. His mother disapproved of some of the things her husband told his children about Padre Martínez. "But he was a great man, Alicia!" his father said.

"He did wonderful things for our people. He was a true hero of the *nuevomexicanos.*"

"A hero, yes," Tony heard his mother murmur. "But no need for you to insist that you're a direct descendant! Saying that he had children doesn't make him any more of a hero. Why do you keep feeding Tony that nonsense?" she demanded in a hushed whisper.

"It's not nonsense," his father said, too loudly. "It's his cultural heritage." Tony's sisters sighed and turned over in their sleep.

"Hush," his mother responded, and that was the end of the conversation.

On the first day of school, when Mr. Wilder had introduced what they were supposed to accomplish for the Heritage Project and how they were each to come up with an individual study project, Tony knew immediately that Padre Martínez would be the most important part of his project.

"This is just the kind of thing I'd hoped you kids would work on, Tony," Mr. Wilder said when Tony told him about Padre Martínez. "You can do all sorts of things with it. You can do an oral presentation, a written report, a poster, a diorama, or a scale model of the Martínez Hacienda. You can bring things from home for a display. We'd take extra good care of them. Maybe your father would be willing to come in and talk to us about your family."

That last suggestion made Tony shudder. He knew how his mother would react to the idea. He wasn't even sure she'd approve of his project. And he didn't want to take a chance on anything wrecking his plans.

Before the day was over, Tony decided to test his idea on Teresa Chávez. Teresa was one of the smartest kids in the class, and he had known her all his life. They grew up in the same neighborhood and went to the same schools from kindergarten on. They even went to the same church.

He remembered when they made their first communion, how pretty Teresa looked in her white dress and veil. She kept her hands clasped under her chin, and her dark brown eyes never wavered from the crucifix above the altar. Meanwhile, most of the boys, including Tony, were fooling around, poking each other, smothering giggles. Now he wanted to show her how he had changed. He hoped it would impress her when he told her about his famous ancestor.

He waited until he saw her coming out of

the cafetorium and fell into step with her. "I've got my plan for the Heritage Project all figured out," he told her, trying not to sound as though he was bragging.

"Yeah? Already?" She shifted her books to her other arm and smoothed the wavy dark hair back from her face.

"I'm going to do it about Padre Martínez of Taos," Tony said, plunging ahead. "See, he's my great-great-something-grandfather, from way way back."

"Who?" She looked totally blank. "I never heard of him."

Tony had grown up hearing so much about Padre Martínez he didn't think he'd have to explain. It was like having to explain who George Washington was. Tony took a deep breath and tried to give her a short history, in about six sentences.

"He's really famous, if you're from Taos," he ended lamely.

"He's a priest? A Catholic priest? And you think he's your grandfather? You got to be joking, Tony."

"Not my actual grandfather. Great-great-great-great—something like that—from way back. I'm named for him."

"Priests don't have kids," she said flatly.

"Well, maybe some did, back then," he persisted.

"I wouldn't brag about it, if I were you," she told him. "It's a sin. You learned that, too, Tony. Remember what Sister Guadalupe said!" Teresa turned and walked away.

Tony felt completely deflated. It hadn't impressed her at all. She even sounded disapproving, like his mother. And what if she was right? What if everybody except his father thought it was a sin, or even that he was making the whole thing up?

In class that afternoon Tony kept worrying about it while the other kids talked about their projects. It was Mr. Wilder's idea that they should all discuss what they were doing and get feedback from other students. *Feedback* was another of Mr. Wilder's favorite words, like *brainstorming*.

Tony envied the kids like Jimmy Ortega who were coming up with ideas that wouldn't make people upset. Jimmy's great-great-uncle was a *santero,* a woodcarver who made little statues of saints. You had to be a very good person and live a very good life, almost like a saint, to do that. Just having talent was not enough. Some of his relative's carvings were in big city museums, Jimmy reported, as far away as Dallas, Texas. Books had even been written about him. He was very old now, Jimmy said, and hardly ever left his village in the mountains.

So Jimmy was descended from a saint, or at least a saintly person who carved statues of saints, while he, Tony, was descended from a sinner. A priest who was a sinner, which was even worse.

For the rest of the day, Tony worried about sin. Now Teresa wouldn't even talk to him, because he was the great-great-great-great-great-grandson of a sinner. It was too late now. He was stuck with his idea. He couldn't think of anything else.

A week later Tony persuaded his father to let him take the picture of Padre Martínez to school. He was planning to use it in a display that would include a map and a poster with a list of some of the things the priest had done. It wasn't an original photograph, just a copy, but his father still warned him to take good care of it.

"It's something you should always cherish," his father said. "He's an ancestor to be proud of. And you're in a direct line, father to son, remember! Not like some of those other relatives, only nephews." Tony was glad his mother wasn't there to hear.

But the beginning of his project started off wrong. On the day Tony was supposed to describe to the class what he was working on, Mr. Wilder was absent, away at some conference, and Ms. Kelsey was substituting. The kids who had come to Rio Grande Middle School in sixth grade remembered Ms. Kelsey and were on edge at her arrival. She had just moved from Ohio to New Mexico the year before, and she didn't seem to like anything about her new home—not the spicy food, not the adobe houses, not even the clumps of *chamisa* that bloomed among the beautiful pink hills. She probably wouldn't like Padre Martínez either.

Tony thought of hiding the portrait and telling her he had forgotten to bring it or making up some other kind of story, but there was his name on the schedule, and Tony felt he had to do something.

Ms. Kelsey loomed over him as he worked on his poster. She raised the little half glasses that hung on a silver chain around her neck and propped them on the end of her nose. "And what is *your* project, Anthony?"

He winced. He hated to be called Anthony.

But Ms. Kelsey didn't believe in using nicknames, and she couldn't seem to pronounce the Spanish names. So Joey became Joseph, Tomás was Thomas, and so on. Tony hoped she didn't expect him to refer to Padre Martínez as Father Anthony Joseph Martinez.

Tony pulled out the portrait and laid it on his desk. Everyone claimed the priest had been so kind and loving, but now the man in this picture looked so fierce!

"It's Padre Antonio José Martínez of Taos," he said in a low voice. "He was a hero to his people."

He was shocked when Ms. Kelsey laughed. "Padre Martinez!" she said. "You're doing your project on that old scoundrel?"

Old scoundrel? Tony stared up at her, his mouth open. He couldn't think what to say. So she knew he was a sinner, too. But that didn't make him a scoundrel, did it? Maybe she had Padre Martínez confused with someone else.

"I just finished reading a book about him," Ms. Kelsey said. "*Death Comes for the Archbishop* by Willa Cather. The author doesn't have a single good thing to say about him. She describes him as having 'long yellow teeth.' He's even rumored to have fathered a number of children. A priest! It's hard to imagine what you would find to admire in a rogue like him, Anthony. You ought to read that book."

Tony was flooded with shame. What was this book she was talking about? Why had his father never mentioned it?

Then Tony heard Teresa's voice, piping up clearly from the back of the room. "Ms. Kelsey, I don't think that book was telling the truth. Padre Martínez was a good man. A really great man. Tony—Anthony," she corrected herself, "has picked a terrific subject. And anyway, maybe there's more to him than got written about in the book you read."

Tony turned around in his seat and gazed at Teresa in amazement. Only a few days ago she'd said she had never even heard of Padre Martínez and insisted Tony couldn't possibly be a descendant. But here she was standing up to Ms. Kelsey! He tried to beam her a message of gratitude, but Teresa didn't even bother to look his way.

"It simply seems to me to be wiser to choose a true hero, rather than someone with a tarnished reputation," Ms. Kelsey insisted. "But then it's not my place to say one way or the other. I'll leave a note for Mr. Wilder about it."

Somehow Tony got through the rest of the day. As soon as school was over, he hurried to find Teresa. "How come you said that?" he asked.

"Because," Teresa said, "I figure you know more about it than Ms. Kelsey does. Especially if you're his great-something-grandson."

"You really believe I am?"

"No. But who cares what happened two hundred years ago? All that matters now is that you say what you believe." Then she smiled at him, a sweet, beautiful smile.

At that moment Tony believed he was walking on air. But it seemed better not to say so.

PADRE MARTÍNEZ, A HERO

❈

by Antonio José Martínez,
a Descendant

THE *first people who lived in New Mexico were Pueblo Indians. In the sixteenth century the Spanish explorers arrived, and for a long time the only people living here were the Indians and the Spanish. Later the Anglo traders came, followed by many more Anglos. Today there are still many people in New Mexico who speak Spanish and keep some of the old customs, like eating beans and tortillas and building adobe houses and having fiestas. Most of them know about Padre Martínez of Taos.*

Antonio José Martínez was born in 1793 in Abiquiú, a little village northwest of Santa Fe. Later his family moved to Taos, farther to the north. His father was a rancher and a businessman, and that's what Antonio José expected to be, too. When he was eighteen years old his father arranged for him to marry a girl named María de la Luz Martín, which means Mary of the Light. A year later they had a baby and named her María de la Luz, too.

But the mother died. Antonio José was very sad when this happened.

He decided to become a priest. He left his baby girl with his parents and traveled to a monastery all the way down in Durango, Mexico, a month's journey on horseback. He studied there for several years. Then he went home to Taos to be a priest. A few years later his little girl died, too, when she was only twelve years old. So he felt very sad again, and to forget his sadness he worked hard for his people.

Here are some things that Padre Martínez did:

He bought a printing press and started publishing books. This was the first real press in New Mexico.

He started a school for girls as well as boys. He taught them in both English and Spanish because he knew they would have to learn how to speak English eventually. This was the first school like it in New Mexico.

He got interested in politics and was elected to represent his people in the government in Mexico and later in the U.S. Territorial government. He was always taking the side of the Hispanic people and the Indians.

He was a good priest. Even after he had a big argument with the new archbishop about church matters and was told he could no longer be a priest, he went on taking care of his people, making sure they got baptized and married and buried. He did this until he died in 1867.

Padre Martínez had children, besides María de la Luz. Some people say that he probably adopted them, or that they were really just his students. Other people believe that he was the actual father of these children. This is what I believe, but whatever anyone believes, no one can say that Padre Martínez was anything but a great man for the people of New Mexico.

PAULINE ROMERO

The Secret of Skinny Bones

You have to tell me a secret," Teresa insisted. "That's what it means to be friends. We trade secrets. You tell me yours, and then I tell you mine."

But Pauline Romero could be as stubborn as Teresa Chávez was determined. "What kind of secret?" Pauline asked.

"Anything, long as it's important."

Pauline thought about it. When her mother moved them to Albuquerque from Santa Clara Pueblo a year ago, Pauline attended the school near their new apartment. The kids at that school weren't mean, but they ignored her as though she wasn't even there. Then she got into the Heritage Project at the

Rio Grande Middle School, where she met Teresa. So far Teresa was the only girl who had gone out of her way to be friendly in this new school. Maybe she did owe her something.

"You go first," she told Teresa.

"I'm thinking about it."

Pauline suspected that Teresa didn't really have a secret either. Then Teresa asked suddenly, "How come you moved here? It must be fun to move. We never moved anyplace."

"It's not so much fun," Pauline admitted. "We did it because my mother got a job. She works at the hospital."

"What about your dad?"

"He didn't come with us. They're divorced," she added. "He moved to another pueblo."

"We don't believe in divorce," Teresa announced. "We're Catholic."

"So are we."

"No, you're not. You're Indian."

"We're both," Pauline explained. "We go to mass on Sundays, and we also have our traditional dances." Maybe she could tell Teresa something about the ceremonial dances— something that sounded like a secret but wasn't really. "We got to be Catholic because of the Spanish conquerors," Pauline said. "Your ancestors, probably," she added pointedly. She could see that Teresa didn't believe her. "Maybe I'll show you sometime. Then you'll see."

The girls reached their health class without anything more being said about secrets. For a while, at least, Pauline didn't have to think of a secret to tell Teresa.

Pauline half-listened to the teacher describing the pyramid of food groups as she doodled on the margins of her notebook with a red ball-point. She liked to sketch designs like the ones her aunt Helen carved on the pots she made to sell to tourists at Indian Market. It was still the beginning of the school year, but Pauline had already filled almost every square inch of the brown inside-out grocery-bag jackets she made to cover her school books.

During the week Pauline lived in a small apartment near the hospital where her mother worked, and on weekends they went to stay with her grandparents at Santa Clara. They lived in the old part of the pueblo below the church, and they had a garden near the river for growing corn and squash and beans. In the yard next to their adobe house was an *horno,* an adobe oven shaped like a beehive, where they baked fat, round loaves of bread. Nothing in the world tasted as good as that bread! Thinking about it made Pauline glad the weekend was coming soon and they'd be going up again.

For the past year Pauline and her family had driven to Santa Clara almost every weekend, unless her mother had to work an extra shift or her sisters managed to talk their mother into staying in the city. Lynnette and Jeannette were in high school where there was always a lot going on—parties, football games, boys. "Better than Española High School," they said, although Pauline thought they must sometimes feel as homesick as she did for their old home at the pueblo.

The older girls bickered constantly with their mother. "I'm so glad you're not at that stage, Pauline," her mother would say.

"Just wait," Lynnette would snap back. She could be mean as a snake when she wanted to. "Skinny Bones is going to be worse than both of us put together. Just because she's so quiet, you think she's good. You're in for a big surprise, Ma."

Pauline never knew what to say when they teased her, calling her Skinny Bones. "Not skinny, delicate," her mother said, sticking up for her, but that made her sisters howl with laughter.

Her sisters always seemed to know exactly

what to say. They talked a lot about how they were going to get away from New Mexico the minute they finished school. One day it was Denver, where they had been once, and the next day it was someplace exciting like Los Angeles or New York, where they had never been. But never back to the pueblo.

"Who wants to hang around there?" they'd say, sounding bored. "Except you, Skinny Bones."

Her sisters were right about that. Pauline never dreamed of living someplace far away; her dream was to move back to Santa Clara and make pots. They called it Kha p'o in the Tewa language—"Valley of the Wild Roses." She couldn't say what it was that drew her there. Even her mother didn't encourage her. "You need to get a good education," her mother would remind her. "That's the important thing."

Her mother sometimes persuaded Lynnette and Jeannette to go up on the weekends by letting them drive. They took turns behind the wheel of the old Ford, while their mother sat in back with Pauline, calling out, "Watch out for that car! Slow down!"

"Backseat driver!" her sisters hollered.

Pauline quietly waited for the trip to end— it could take almost two hours if traffic was heavy—and for the other half of her life to resume. On the way up to Santa Clara she thought about school and whatever had happened that week in the Heritage Project class, her favorite. On the way back to the city she thought about what had happened at the pueblo over the weekend. Back and forth she traveled between her two worlds, R. G. School and Kha p'o.

• • •

One weekend last winter Pauline's aunt Helen, who was one of the best-known potters in a pueblo noted for its gleaming black and lustrous red pottery, had handed her a lump of clay and said, "Here, Pauline, see what you can do with this. Watch me."

Her aunt's fingers seemed to speak to the clay, and the clay answered with a wonderful shape. But when Pauline tried—even with a simple bowl smaller than the palm of her hand—the pot fell apart before she had really gotten started. The clay would not answer.

"Keep trying," Aunt Helen said.

Pauline's sisters sighed when their aunt offered them lumps of clay. "It takes too long," Lynnette complained. "Isn't there a faster way to do it?" Jeannette asked.

"Lots of faster ways," Aunt Helen told them. "But not good ways."

After months of practice Pauline's fingers slowly began to learn the language of clay. Gradually a pot grew from coils thick as her finger that she wound around and around. It was small and plain, with straight sides and hardly any rim, but it was a pot.

Aunt Helen specialized in black wedding vases with twin spouts joined by a handle. The narrow spouts were tricky to shape and difficult to rub to a rich luster, but the vases were a popular item among tourists who paid high prices for them. Pauline didn't see how she'd ever be able to make anything so beautiful.

Pauline's mother had once made some pots, when she was a younger woman, but after the divorce she went to school and learned how to take blood samples from patients. That was the end of making pots. Making a living for her girls was more important.

Her mother had tried to get a job in Española or in Santa Fe, which at least wasn't too far away, but the only work she could find was in Albuquerque, almost ninety miles from the pueblo. So the four of them moved into a small apartment. Pauline shared a fold-out bed in the living room with her mother so her sisters could have the bedroom. The view from their windows was the parking lot of a Lota

Burger, where her sisters worked part-time.

When school in Albuquerque let out at the end of May, Aunt Helen said to Pauline, "Would you like to stay up here with me this summer and make pots?"

Would she! "Oh, yes!"

Aunt Helen's home was in the new part of the pueblo, across the bridge from the church. She made pots in her living room and fired them in the backyard. The summer weeks passed quickly, but Pauline's pots went slowly. There were so many steps! Finally she completed her first pot and put it with her aunt's to be fired. When the firing was finished, Pauline's little pot lay in pieces. She stared at it, near tears. But her aunt had also lost one of the wedding vases.

"Those pots were not meant to be," Aunt Helen said with a shrug. "We try again. That's all you can do."

The next time they fired, Pauline put in two pots, and both came out whole. "Sign your name on the bottom and we'll set them on the table on the feast day when lots of tourists come. Maybe somebody will buy them." They decided to ask fifteen dollars for each of Pauline's pots. Pauline couldn't believe anyone would actually pay that much.

Santa Clara Pueblo celebrated its feast day, the biggest occasion of the year, on August twelfth. Early that month one of the men in the village visited Aunt Helen's husband, Larry, and asked his permission for Pauline to dance the sacred dances. Pauline was thrilled—she had never danced before. Every day Pauline went to the kiva, the sacred ceremonial chamber, to learn the dance of the Winter People.

Traditionally, half the people of the pueblo belonged to the Summer People, who performed ceremonial dances relating to planting and harvest, and the other half were Winter People, whose dances were usually about animals and hunting. Sometimes the dancers imitated deer or buffalo. These were Pauline's favorites. Whether you were born Summer or Winter depended not on your birthday but on what your father was. Pauline belonged to the Winter People. For the feast day they would do a Harvest Dance.

Aunt Helen was not going to dance. She would be busy selling pots. "I'll look after your pots for you, Pauline," she promised. "You dance for me."

Pauline's mother took part of her vacation from the hospital and came up a few days ahead of time. The morning of the feast day, she helped Pauline get ready.

Pauline loved her costume, which had belonged to one of Aunt Helen's grown-up daughters: a heavy manta dress woven of white wool, the hem embroidered with black, green, and red designs; and a lace-trimmed blue shawl fastened on one shoulder with a beautiful silver pin. The soft white moccasins came up to her knees. She wore a *tablita,* a wooden headdress carved and painted with symbols of ears of corn, and she carried an evergreen branch in one hand and an ear of corn in the other.

Everything the dancers wore had a special meaning. The men of the Winter People wore white shirts and white kilts with crocheted leggings. They danced with rain sashes tied around their waists, the long fringes representing the rain so important to a corn crop.

On the morning of the feast day everyone attended mass in the church. After mass the statue of Santa Clara, in whose honor the pueblo was named, was carried from the church down the hill to the outdoor shrine in the main plaza of the old part of the village. Pauline and the other dancers entered the kiva through a hole in the roof and waited. When they heard the drummers begin their soft, rhythmic beat, they climbed up the ladder to the roof of the kiva and descended onto the plaza, an open area surrounded by clusters of small adobe houses. The singers, a group of men who knew the ancient rituals, began to sing.

They sang in Tewa, the language spoken at most of the pueblos in this part of the Rio Grande Valley. At Taos Pueblo to the north, the language was Tiwa, a little bit different, and at Jémez Pueblo a few miles to the southwest, the people spoke Towa, and that was a little bit different, too. But all were derived from the same language, Tanoan. At the pueblos south of Albuquerque where Pauline's father lived with his new wife, the people spoke a language totally different from Tanoan. Pueblo people had much in common, and yet each pueblo had its own way of speaking, its own way of making and decorating clay pots, its own way of performing ceremonial dances.

Some of the ceremonies were secret. Pauline knew, for example, that certain secret things would happen in her finishing ceremony, her rite of passage to adulthood, but she had no idea what those secrets were. Her sisters, who had already been through the ceremony, refused to tell her. "It's not such a big deal," they said with a shrug sometimes, and at other times, when they wanted to tease her, they'd pretend it was something terrifying, like having to stay out alone all night—naked, without even a blanket—up on the old cliffs where their ancestors had once lived. She tried not to believe them.

Pauline listened to the words of the singers and the message of the drum and concentrated on keeping her eyes modestly lowered and taking small steps—the boys and men stepped higher, more vigorously, than the women. But her *tablita* slipped to one side, and one of the captains, who kept the crowds of visitors from getting in the way of the dancers, came over and straightened the awkward headdress for her. More than a hundred people danced, from old people to small children—two parallel lines snaking through the plaza. On and on the dancing went under the blazing August sun.

When the song ended, Pauline's group of Winter People moved to a smaller plaza not far from the main plaza to repeat their dance. Wherever she looked, white people had crowded into the pueblo that was usually so quiet and peaceful! Pauline glanced around for Lynnette, who had promised to bring her a drink of water between dances. But Lynnette was talking to a tall Anglo with an expensive video camera propped on his shoulder. He was blocking the view of some of the old people who sat on lawn chairs in a shrinking scrap of shade, and her sister was telling him to move.

"They act like we're some kind of side-show," Lynnette always complained about the visitors who poured into the village. "They stare and they ask more dumb questions than you can even imagine, like 'When are they gonna come out in those big war bonnets?' like we were Plains Indians. And they don't even know the difference between us and the Navajo."

Jeannette always took the other side. She loved the tourists. She hung around hoping one would notice her and offer her a job in Hollywood. She speculated about where they came from in their big new cars and hoped someday she'd have a car and flashy clothes and a fancy camera, too.

Aunt Helen was practical. "If they have money, they buy pots. Maybe they'll buy one of my pots, or one of yours, Pauline. If you work hard and you're good and you're also lucky, then one of your pots goes with them, and their money stays here."

"I cannot believe how rude some of these people are," Lynnette grumbled when she finally showed up with Pauline's water. "That guy with the camera offered me a dollar to take him inside the kiva. Can you imagine that?"

Pauline sighed. Anglos didn't understand that the kiva was the sacred place of worship, and if you weren't one of the People, you weren't allowed to go in there.

The sun was setting when the dances ended and most of the tourists had driven off in their cars and RVs. Only a few special visitors were invited to stay for a meal. Pauline's mother had worked all day at Grandmother's, cooking *posole*—hominy stew with lots of chile—and baking bread in the *horno*. The delicious smell had been drifting through the pueblo since early morning. Pauline could hardly wait to get out of her sweaty costume and have something to eat.

But first she ran to Aunt Helen's table in the small plaza by Grandmother's house to see how pottery sales had gone. Helen had sold several of her wedding vases and a couple of seed pots with openings in the top so tiny you could hardly get even the tip of your finger into them. But the two small black pots that Pauline had set out were still there.

"Don't be discouraged," Helen said. "We'll

take them to Indian Market in Santa Fe next weekend. It's a madhouse, but you'll learn a lot."

Indian Market! Pauline knew that was where the best Indian potters and weavers and jewelers took their work to sell. Judges would hand out prize ribbons. Aunt Helen had a collection of blue, red, and yellow ones from previous years. Pauline's pots weren't anywhere near good enough.

"Don't worry," Aunt Helen told her. "It's not our way, this competition for prizes. You should always do your best, whether there's a prize or not. Still, it's good for business, having a blue ribbon hanging on your booth."

Pauline agreed to go, but after only a couple of hours at Aunt Helen's booth on the plaza in Santa Fe, she regretted it. There were too many people, they pressed too close, they asked too many questions. It made her nervous to see how carelessly they handled her aunt's wedding vases, how their rings scratched the polished surfaces. She wished her mother would come and take her home. But Helen talked her into staying. "This is part of making the pot," she said.

By the last day of the market a red ribbon hung on Aunt Helen's booth and most of the wedding vases had been sold, but Pauline's two pots still sat there. Pauline had nearly given up when a woman in a straw hat and a silver-and-turquoise necklace stopped at their booth and noticed the pots. She picked up the one with a zigzag lightning design around the rim and examined it. Then she turned it over and looked at the bottom where Pauline had signed her name and Helen had stuck a tiny sticker with the price. Pauline wondered if the woman would think fifteen dollars was too much to pay for such a small pot, one that was plainly a little bit lopsided. The woman looked carefully at Pauline.

"Did you make this pot?"

Pauline nodded.

" 'Pauline Romero,' " she read. "How old are you, Pauline?"

"Twelve."

"Who taught you to make pots?"

"My aunt." Pauline gestured toward Aunt Helen.

The woman pulled a leather wallet out of her handbag. "Fifteen dollars seems like a fair price," she said, laying a ten and a five on the counter right in front of Pauline. "Next year I'll look for this booth again, and I'll buy another pot. I'll buy one every year until I have a whole collection of pots by Pauline Romero and you're famous and your pots are exhibited in a museum." She tucked Pauline's little black pot in her big handbag, smiled, and walked away.

That was in August, and Pauline had been thinking about the woman and her pot ever since, going over and over in her mind that special moment when she *knew*. It was the secret she finally decided to tell Teresa, something she had told no one else.

The next time Teresa asked, Pauline was ready. "An Anglo lady is going to buy one of my pots every year," she said. "She says someday they'll be in a museum, and I'll be famous. So my secret is I'm going to be a potter."

Pauline waited while Teresa pondered whether or not that was a good secret. Teresa narrowed her eyes at Pauline. "No one else knows this?"

Pauline shook her head. She hadn't even told her mother, who hoped she would be a nurse or even a doctor.

"All right then," Teresa announced. "And now I'll tell you my secret." She motioned for Pauline to lean closer. "I'm a witch," Teresa whispered. "Not *going* to be. Am already."

HOW TO MAKE A POT

✦

Interview with Helen López
by Pauline Romero

YOU *ask me, how do I make a pot, and I tell you that my whole life is about making a pot. There are so many little things that I learned to do, and I don't think about it anymore. It would take a whole book, to write it all down.*

But anyway, you have to start with the clay. My husband digs it from the fields near the river at our pueblo and brings it to our house. I crumble up the clay and mix it with water in a big washtub. Every day for a couple of weeks I stir it around to get out the little sticks and stones. Every day I pour dirty water out and clean water in. When the clay is clean, I add volcanic sand or old broken pots that I've ground up fine. This is called temper and keeps the pots from cracking as they dry. Then I start mixing. You can use your hands or maybe your feet. All of this takes a long time. And it's so much hard work.

All right, now I have my clay and I'm ready to shape my pot. Pueblo people shape our pots by hand. We never use a wheel. You lay out a clay base and put it on a puki, *which can be a plate or pie tin, anything to hold it flat. If it's only a tiny pot, you just hold it in your hand.*

Then you roll out a coil of clay about as thick as your thumb and start winding it around and around on the base. You keep turning the pot and building up the wall, one coil on top of the other, shaping the pot with your fingers and pressing and squeezing the coils to get out all the air bubbles that would make the pot explode when it's fired.

As you go along, you scrape the wall of the pot with a piece of gourd or maybe a spoon until it's so smooth you can't even tell the pot was made from coils. You make the walls thick or thin, depending on how you plan to decorate it.

Now you want to know, how do I decorate the pot? When the clay has dried as hard as leather— and that depends on weather, rainy or dry—I carve a design in the pot with a knife. Melon pots are deeply carved with ribs to resemble a melon, and my wedding vases have beautiful carved designs. Then I set the pot aside again. After it is completely dry, it is sanded smooth. I enjoy decorating the pot, but sanding is always a mess! I try to do that outdoors.

After that we burnish the pot to make it shiny. Our people don't use glazes, you know! First I paint on a thin coat of watered-down clay called slip, and while the slip is still damp, I rub it with a polishing stone. Our polishing stones are very precious to us—I have the one my grandmother used. I wouldn't part with it for anything! I rub and rub with the stone until the pot has an even shine. You have to be careful because if you rub too hard, you might go right through the slip, and then you have to sand off all the slip and start over. I've had to do that many times. Melon pots are hard to burnish because you have to rub in the deep grooves between the ribs. And my wedding vases are hard because the necks and handles are so fragile. One wrong move and—snap!

Not all designs are carved. There are also painted designs and etched designs, and they're both done after the pot is burnished. You paint on the design with slip. Slip that isn't burnished stays dull when it's fired, so there's a contrast between the shiny burnished surface and the dull matte surface. There's another way to decorate a pot: you can cut very fine lines through the dried slip. This is called etching.

Whether it's carved or painted or etched, we use all kinds of designs, some traditional, some modern. I like the old designs: the serpent, or the lightning symbol, or the four sacred mountains of the pueblo people, or a bear. Long ago during a terrible drought when the river was dry and the springs were empty, a bear showed one of our medicine men where to find water. Since then we have honored the bear who saved our people.

All of this takes hours and hours of work, so many I can't count, maybe four or five weeks altogether! But then the pot is ready to be fired, and that's exciting. Firing takes the least amount of time, only about an hour. All of us potters look forward to this part through those weeks of work. We build our own kilns to fire the pots. We rig up a kiln in the yard every time we fire. Each potter has a different way of doing it. You pick a day when the wind isn't blowing. You put your pots in a child's wagon or some kind of metal box, which is then set on top of tin cans in the yard with other metal things, like old bedsprings and pieces of sheet metal, arranged all around the pots to keep the fire from actually touching them. You pile wood and bark and dried cow patties on top of the bedsprings and under the wagon, so your fire burns all around and the pots are inside the fire. What happens next depends on whether you want your pottery to turn out red or black.

Here's what I mean by this: Whether you get a red pot or a black pot depends on how you fire it—it's all the same clay. If you rake away the burned wood and cow patties at the end of the firing and pull out the pots, you will have dark red pottery. But if you dump enough dried-out, ground-up horse manure on the fire to smother it, that keeps air from reaching the pots, and the clay turns black. The first time I fired a pot, I couldn't believe it. Like magic or something.

So then, when the fire cools down, you scrape away the ashes, move the metal out of the way, and hope your pots are all right. If something went wrong—if there was an air bubble or a little crack you didn't notice beforehand—the pot breaks and there you are with nothing. It's hard not to feel sad when you work so hard for so long on just one pot. But I believe these pots were not meant to be, and losing a pot is one of the things you just have to learn.

This is how we've been making pots at Santa Clara Pueblo for hundreds of years.

TERESA CHÁVEZ

❖

Curing Ms. Kelsey

T ERESA CHÁVEZ knew she never
should have told Pauline Romero
about being a witch. Better to tell her that
Abuelita, her grandmother, had promised to
teach Teresa to be a *curandera,* a "healer." But
that didn't sound nearly as dramatic.

For as long as Teresa could remember,
Abuelita had been healing people—not just
members of her own family but friends and
neighbors and even strangers who came to see
her. Most of the time she would cure them by
giving them herb teas that made them feel
better. But not all of Abuelita's *remedios,* "remedies," were done with herbs. Some ailments

couldn't be cured by just giving a warm liquid to drink. There was more to it than that.

One day last summer Teresa was in the supermarket with her mother and two little brothers: Carlito strapped in the kiddy seat of the shopping cart; Roberto hunched up on the bottom shelf. Teresa walked beside them, pulling off the shelves whatever her mother asked for, or staying with the two boys while her mother went off in search of something in another aisle.

Roberto, who was seven, tried to sneak cookies and Count Chocula cereal into the basket as soon as their mother's back was turned. But Carlito was still a baby, too young to be troublesome. He had big green eyes and pretty golden curls and the most adorable smile. (Teresa's hair and eyes were dark, and so were Roberto's. She often thought she'd like to get green contact lenses when she was older.) People were always making a fuss over Carlito, saying what a beautiful child he was. Mama had warned Teresa to be careful of that.

"Watch out for strangers," Mama said. "They can give him the *mal ojo,* the evil eye. Somebody who covets him, really wants him for themselves, can give him the *mal ojo* just by saying how pretty he is. Make sure they touch him. If the person goes away without touching him, Carlito could get real sick. You can die from the *mal ojo,* you know."

Teresa watched, and sure enough all the people who stopped to admire Carlito made a point of touching the baby lightly on the arm or the back, so nothing bad happened.

While Teresa was trying to keep Roberto from smuggling forbidden sweets aboard the shopping cart, a woman in a flowing dress stopped and began making the usual noises over Carlito. Her frizzy gray hair stuck out in all directions, her eyes were as pale as her hair, and her silver earrings flashed when she bent down to fuss over the little boy.

"He's simply gorgeous," the woman cooed. "He looks like a Botticelli angel!"

A moment later the woman was gone, sweeping down the aisle as though a breeze was blowing her along. But, too late, Teresa realized she hadn't touched the baby. Had she tried to give him the *mal ojo?* The woman was an Anglo—maybe she didn't know she had to touch him. And maybe if you were an Anglo and didn't know, then you couldn't give somebody the evil eye. Teresa decided not to say anything to her mother. *After all,* Teresa thought, *I might be mistaken.*

65

But the next day Carlito, always so bubbly and good-natured, seemed cranky. He threw his bottle out of his crib, which he never did, and then cried for it. While he was sleeping, Teresa crept into the room he shared with Roberto and touched his face. It definitely felt hot.

Teresa was afraid her mother would blame her. "Why did you let her do it?" Mama would ask. "Why didn't you run after her and tell her she had to touch the baby after she admired him? Why didn't you come and get me?" Teresa didn't have the answers, so she kept quiet.

When Carlito got up from his nap, Mama noticed he had developed a slight fever. "Get Abuelita," Mama said.

Teresa ran across the street to find her grandmother, relieved to have been given something to do. "Carlito's sick," Teresa explained. "Just a little fever." She hoped that's all it was.

Teresa's short, plump *abuela* bustled into her back room, where bunches of drying herbs hung from the ceiling, and chose a glass jar from one of the long shelves. "We start with this," she told Teresa, showing her the gnarled, brown root in the jar.

But the bitter-tasting tea that Abuelita brewed from the root, sweetened with a lump of *piloncillo,* and gently coaxed Carlito to drink a sip at a time didn't seem to help. By evening he was worse. Papa wanted to call the doctor, but Mama persuaded him to wait a little longer. "Abuelita can help him," she said. "We must let her try."

Teresa knew she had to say something. When her parents left the house on an errand, Teresa seized her chance. *"Mal ojo,"* she whispered so softly her grandmother made her repeat it, and Teresa, trying not to cry, explained what had happened.

"You should have told me sooner," Abuelita said gently. "But don't worry. We'll sweep him. It will be all right, *mi hijita.*" She sent Teresa to bring her a raw egg and a blue china saucer from Mama's good set. "Watch carefully, Teresita," she said.

Carlito lay in his crib, gazing up at them with eyes bright with fever. Abuelita stepped up to the crib, and holding the raw egg with the tips of her fingers, she passed it slowly over his body, up and down, back and forth, sweeping him with the egg. Then Abuelita took the saucer, broke the egg into it in one deft motion, and set the saucer on the floor beneath the crib.

"Now bring me a glass of water," she said, "and tell me as much as you can remember about this woman who caused our Carlito harm."

Teresa brought the water and once again described the woman in the supermarket. For the cure to be really effective, the woman with the wild gray hair should have been there, too. Since she wasn't, Abuelita would have to take her place. Grandmother shut her eyes, wrinkled her brow as though she was thinking hard, and took a sip of water. Carefully she brushed her wet lips over Carlito's hot cheeks. She did it a second time and a third, leaving a wet trail on his face.

"All right," she said, stepping back. "He'll be fine now."

And the next morning Carlito was indeed much better, standing in his crib, crowing like a little rooster, and calling for his "baba," his bottle.

Teresa remembered the raw egg in the dish beneath his crib. When she bent to pick it up, she saw that something like an eye had formed on the bright yellow yolk, the dark pinpoint of a pupil surrounded by a hazy, lighter-colored iris. Silently she took it to her grandmother, who was not in the least surprised. "Pour it on the ground near my peach tree," she instructed.

From then on, Teresa listened carefully as her *abuela* talked to her about herbs, where to find them, how to dry them, how to brew teas with them, what they could do. "I'll teach you all I know," Abuelita promised. "You'll learn to cure people. Already you know how to cure the *mal ojo,* right, *mi hijita?*"

Teresa nodded.

"It's God's will that your beautiful little brother got well," Abuelita continued. "I've been chosen by God, you see. He put me here on earth to heal. He gave me *el don,* the gift, in these two hands. He also gave me *el don* here"—she pointed to her head—"and most of all, right here." She laid her plump hand over her heart. "Perhaps you have been chosen, too, Teresita!"

The notion of being chosen by God made Teresa feel cold and shivery. It was a scary idea, being chosen.

"Sometimes when you get sick, it may be because El Diablo has a hold on some part of you, and that causes things to go wrong inside. But a good *curandera* can shake the Devil loose and send him straight back to hell! You have to believe, too. It doesn't work if you don't believe, deep down in your soul, that it will work."

. . .

Teresa remembered that incident with Carlito when she got the idea of doing something about Ms. Kelsey, the sub at R. G. School. Something had to be done. Maybe, Teresa thought, she could put the *mal ojo* on the teacher who still pronounced her name "Tuh-REE-suh shah-VEZ" instead of the Spanish way, "Teh-RAY-sah CHAH-vess" and seemed to think Ohio was so much better than New Mexico.

Teresa consulted her grandmother. "Could you teach me how to put a spell on somebody? Somebody who's mean?"

"Mean to you, *mi hijita?* Who could ever be mean to a sweet girl like you?" Abuelita asked.

"I can't say exactly who. And not just to me. To lots of people." Maybe *mean* wasn't the right word, but Teresa couldn't think of a better one.

"Well," her grandmother said, thinking it over, "I believe you're talking about an evil spell, which would be a very bad thing, very serious. You have to be a *bruja,* a real witch, to do something like that. But," she went on, "maybe you're thinking about it backward."

"Backward?"

"Maybe whoever this person is who seems so mean already has a spell on him, or her, and that's what's causing the trouble. This person doesn't need to get a spell. This person needs to have the spell taken away, the way we got rid of Carlito's *mal ojo.*"

This was a new one to Teresa. Suppose someone had actually put a spell on Ms. Kelsey back in Ohio so that she saw only the bad things and never saw the good ones? She said chile gave her a stomachache, and she thought the earth-colored adobe houses were "bleak," and it bothered her that it was too dry to grow a nice green lawn like the one she had back home in Cincinnati. The worst thing, though, was the way she mispronounced Spanish names and words. She seemed like a foreigner, an alien from another planet. Poor thing!

The more Teresa thought about it, the more she liked the idea of trying to cure Ms. Kelsey and make her *like* being in New Mexico. But since they never knew exactly when the sub was going to be there, Teresa would have to be patient and wait for her chance.

Usually if it was Teresa's turn to hand in a paper or make an oral report, anything that made her nervous, she could count on Ms. Kelsey being there. But it was on the day that Teresa's friend Pauline was to give a report in class on Indian dances that Ms. Kelsey appeared again in Mr. Wilder's place. Teresa became extraordinarily alert as Pauline stepped in front of the class. She was sure Ms. Kelsey would say something without even meaning to that would make Pauline curl up inside.

Pauline started her description of the feast day. "I'm one of the Winter People," she said, "and I wore my white manta dress and my *tablita* and carried an ear of corn. We danced all day. Then a lot of my relatives came and we had a big dinner."

When Pauline had finished her report, Ms. Kelsey spoke up. "Very nice, Pauline," she said. "I must confess I've never understood what those dances are all about. The one time I went with friends we had to wait such a long time for the dances to begin because nothing started on time. And then a very rude man came around and took away my friend's tape recorder and said it wasn't allowed. We were quite upset by that."

"But the songs are sacred," Pauline blurted out.

Teresa thought she saw tears in Pauline's eyes. *That's it,* she decided, watching her friend sit down abruptly without saying another word; *something's got to be done about Ms. Kelsey. Now!*

Teresa waited restlessly while the others gave their reports about special family celebrations, hardly hearing a word of what they said about their Thanksgivings and Christmases and Jeremy's description of Passover. When the bell rang for lunch, Teresa slipped out of the side door by the cafetorium and ran all the way home. She knew she wasn't supposed to leave school during the day without a written permission slip from her mother, and she also knew she'd never be able to fake one they'd believe. But she figured if she got caught, that was just one more problem to solve.

No one was at home, of course—her parents were at work, Roberto in school, and Carlito at day care. Teresa grabbed an egg out of the refrigerator and made a nest of paper towels in an empty milk carton. Then she found the pretty blue china saucer her *abuela* had used, tucked it in next to the egg, and

73

rushed back to school, arriving just as the bell rang for her fifth-period class. Her stomach rumbling with hunger and nervousness, she scooted into her seat and set the milk carton on the floor between her feet.

Ms. Kelsey took forever to give the class an assignment on clouds and weather, but at last the sub sat down and bent over a stack of papers on the teacher's desk. Teresa slid the egg out of its nest and cradled it in one hand, the blue saucer in the other. Cautiously she made her way across the room, in the general direction of the pencil sharpener, keeping the egg and saucer out of sight. Ms. Kelsey glanced up but then went back to her papers.

Teresa glided past and stopped directly behind the teacher. Holding her breath and trying not to squeeze the fragile egg too hard, Teresa swept the egg over Ms. Kelsey's back and head and shoulders. Teresa wished she could include the teacher's legs and feet, too. It would be better to do it slowly, giving the egg yolk plenty of chance to soak up all of Ms. Kelsey's *foreignness,* her special kind of *mal ojo,* but she was afraid to risk it. Franklyn Cox and Jimmy Ortega and Pauline were all staring at her.

The first part, the sweeping, was done, but

now came a harder part. You couldn't break an egg in a silent classroom without somebody noticing!

"Yes, Teresa?" Ms. Kelsey said, turning around so quickly Teresa barely had time to hide the egg and saucer behind her back. "What is it?"

"Nothing," Teresa stammered. "I was just going to look out the window at the clouds. For my weather report," she added.

"I believe you can see them just as well from your seat," Ms. Kelsey said. "Now please sit down." She turned back to her papers.

"Yes, ma'am." But Teresa didn't move. She stood still, trying to work up her courage.

At that moment Jimmy rose in his seat to get a better look at what Teresa was up to and managed to knock over his desk with a tremendous clatter. Ms. Kelsey jumped and let out a little shriek. Teresa quickly cracked the shell on the edge of the blue saucer and slid the egg into it. While Franklyn helped Jimmy set his desk upright, Teresa shoved the saucer with the glistening raw egg under the teacher's desk.

Jimmy slumped in his seat, red-faced, the class went back to work, and Ms. Kelsey sat back down in her chair. Only Pauline stared at Teresa, her mouth a wide O. Casual as a cat strolling down an alley, Teresa went back to her seat and crammed the sticky pieces of eggshell inside the desk. She gave Pauline a big smile.

According to Abuelita, the egg was supposed to stay under the person's bed overnight. But before the end of school that day Teresa would have to figure out a way to retrieve the egg from under the desk. It was possible that the cure wouldn't work at all under these strange circumstances, but if it worked even a little bit, if Ms. Kelsey showed the slightest improvement, it would be a success. A couple of hours was probably better than nothing. Teresa opened her workbook and stared at cloud formations—big, fluffy ones and flat, thin ones.

Clink! Teresa shut her eyes and waited for what would come next.

"What?" the teacher gasped, peering under the desk where her foot had hit the saucer.

If she leaned to the right, Teresa could see the bright yellow yolk swimming in the slimy swirl of clear egg white on the tile floor. Everybody crowded forward to see, but Ms. Kelsey waved them back. "It seems to be a . . . a raw egg." Several people giggled out loud. "All right," Ms. Kelsey said grimly. "What is this supposed to be about?"

The teacher's sharp eyes darted up and down the rows of students, nailing each one like a board in a fence. When the piercing look paused on her, Teresa licked her dry lips and leaned forward. "Uh," she began.

"Yes, Tuh-REE-suh? You know something about this?"

"Well, it's my egg. And my mother's saucer. It's an experiment," she rattled on, "I didn't mean for you to step on it or to make a mess. But I guess it didn't work."

"I should say it didn't," Ms. Kelsey said coldly.

"What kind of an experiment?" Franklyn asked, waving his hand. Teresa could have killed him. She didn't want to have to answer any questions.

Ms. Kelsey glowered. "And? I'm sure we'd all like to hear your explanation."

Teresa's mind whirled like a windmill. "It's kind of a . . . a *weather* experiment," she said, suddenly inspired. "See, if you put an egg in a saucer on the floor and leave it overnight and an eye forms in it, that means there's going to be a bad storm. Ummm . . . then you take the egg outside and bury it in the backyard, and that takes away the power of the storm."

"I see," said Ms. Kelsey. "And you really believe that, Tuh-REE-suh?"

Teresa shrugged. It actually sounded like a pretty good idea.

"I see," Ms. Kelsey said again, in a tone that made it plain that she didn't see at all. "It seems to me that you're telling us about a *superstition,* not a scientific experiment. In any event, Tuh-REE-suh," she continued, "I would appreciate your cleaning up the mess under my desk since you haven't been able to predict any change in the weather. And let's all the rest of us get back to our work, shall we?"

Down on her hands and knees, Teresa tried to scoop the slippery mess back into the saucer with a paper towel. The yolk, amazingly, was still intact. For a moment she thought she saw a dark pupil and the faint ring of an iris. But as she stared at it, they seemed to disappear. On the way to the girls' bathroom, she hesitated. With or without the *ojo,* this egg wasn't supposed to be flushed down the sewer.

For the second time that day, Teresa sneaked out the side door to the schoolyard.

She poured the eggy mess on the spot where they were digging up the place to put the new school sign. The way things were going, she was not surprised when a hall monitor, an eighth-grade girl, spotted her. "What are you doing out here?" the girl asked.

"Dumping a mess, is all," Teresa explained, wiping her sticky hands on her pants. "Ms. Kelsey sent me."

"Oh, do you have her?" the girl said. "She's kind of strange."

"She's not so bad," Teresa said, amazed to hear this coming out of her mouth. "Actually she can be pretty nice." She remembered what Abuelita had told her: you have to believe it's going to work.

The hall monitor let her go with a warning, and Teresa stopped by the girls' bathroom to wash the china saucer. Then she remembered there was one more part to the cure: you had to sprinkle water on the person with your mouth. Wishing it were all over, Teresa got a mouthful of water from the drinking fountain. She hoped Ms. Kelsey wouldn't ask her a question before she had a chance to do the next part.

Careful not to swallow and trying to keep the water from dribbling down her chin,

Teresa tiptoed up behind Ms. Kelsey. Then she glanced at Pauline who had such a strange look on her face that Teresa started to laugh and sputtered instead. There went the water, spraying all over the back of Ms. Kelsey's dress.

As Ms. Kelsey spun around, Teresa reached out and touched her. That was the last thing—touching the person. "Teresa!" she said. "What am I going to do with you today!"

She heard it! She was sure she heard it. Ms. Kelsey had said Teh-RAY-sah, instead of Tuh-REE-suh. Surely everybody else had heard it, too. "I'm sorry, Ms. Kelsey," she said. "I really am."

When the dismissal bell rang, Teresa ran to catch up with Pauline. "Did you hear her?" Teresa asked excitedly.

"Hear what? You were really getting in her face today, for sure."

"She called me Teh-RAY-sah. Didn't you hear her?"

"Isn't that what she always calls you?"

Teresa made a face. "She doesn't pronounce it right, usually. She makes it sound like a *gringa* name."

"But she's a *gringa!* What do you expect?

Next you'll be wanting her to speak Tewa."

Teresa was not discouraged. She had heard Ms. Kelsey right, she was sure. This was the first sign. The cure had worked. Ms. Kelsey was rid of the spell. Pretty soon now she was going to change. Buy an Indian pot and start wearing turquoise jewelry. Admire adobe houses. Tell them how much she enjoyed enchiladas. Pronounce all the Spanish names right. It had already started.

You just had to believe the cure would work. Teresa knew it would.

HABLA ESPAÑOL AQUÍ

"(SOME) SPANISH IS SPOKEN HERE"

❖

by Teresa Chávez

RÍO GRANDE *means "Big River" in Spanish. It should never be called Rio Grande River because* rio *is Spanish for "river," and that would be like saying Big River River. Some people pronounce it "REE-oh GRAND" and others say "REE-oh GRAN-dee." Spanish-speaking people say "REE-oh GRAHN-day," which is probably most correct. Our school is named for this historical body of water.*

The river was given its name by Spanish explorers who came in the sixteenth century looking for gold. But instead the explorers found Pueblo Indians who knew a lot about farming and irrigation but had no gold. Eventually other Spanish people came and settled in this area, which was then part of Mexico. At that time Mexico belonged to Spain and was called New Spain. Mexico achieved independence from Spain in 1821, and New Mexico was a province. Then the U.S. Army arrived in 1846 and made New Mexico a territory of the United States. Lots of Anglos came as traders along the Santa Fe Trail during that century. An Anglo is anybody who is not Hispanic or Native American.

About half the people living in New Mexico are of Hispanic ancestry. Many New Mexicans speak Spanish, and a lot of the names of people and places in New Mexico are Spanish. For instance, Albuquerque was named for the Duke of Alburquerque, a Spaniard. But there is a story that when the railroad reached the town the Anglo stationmaster couldn't speak Spanish and by mistake left out the first r of Alburquerque, making it Albuquerque. *Santa Fe* means "holy faith." Even our mountains have Spanish names: *Sangre de Cristo* means "Blood of Christ," and *Sandía*, the name of the mountains in Albuquerque, means "watermelon." Both of these names are because the mountains turn deep pink or red every evening at sunset.

There are also many Indian names, like Abiquiú, where the famous painter Georgia O'Keeffe lived, Chimayó, Taos, and Pojoaque. One town with a strange name is Truth or Consequences, in southern New Mexico. It was originally called *Aguas Calientes* and later given the English name of Hot Springs. Then it was renamed for a radio show from the 1950s.

We have put a pronunciation guide for names and places and often-used words at the end of this book to help people who want to pronounce our beautiful Spanish language correctly.

APRIL ELLIS

❧

April's Mud

April ELLIS thought the best thing about going to a new school was nobody knew—*yet!*—that she lived in a converted school bus painted lavender, orange, and green and parked in a weed-grown lot near the Rio Grande.

April had figured that once her grandparents had gone home to Philadelphia after their yearly visit over Labor Day, her family would get back to their "normal" life again. The last thing Nana said to April's parents as she climbed aboard the Amtrak train headed east was, "For the sake of the children, if not for yourselves, *please* give up this . . . this hippie life!" They had made it plain for seven days that what April's family considered normal wasn't "normal" at all. Not to Nana and Poppy. "Normal," April now realized, was a matter of opinion.

Nana and Poppy weren't the only ones who thought her parents were hippies. April had heard people talking about them at her old school. Most people born in the 1950s, as her parents had been, had "gotten it all out of their system" (Poppy's phrase) and gone back to whatever they had dropped out of, cut their hair, shaved their beards, and put on suits and ties and all the rest.

But not Susan and Tom Ellis. (April called them Susan and Tom, not Mom and Dad.) Tom still had a scraggly beard, and his idea of getting dressed up was to put on clean overalls and tie his long, wheat-colored hair back in a ponytail.

Susan was truly beautiful, in April's opinion. Her thick, wiry hair had turned gray early and framed her thin face in a silvery halo. Her pale eyes were silvery, too, and she loved to wear bright clothes that fluttered when she walked and silver jewelry that flashed from her ears and jangled on her wrists.

Tom, who was very good with his hands, had bought the school bus a few years earlier when they decided to leave California and move to the Southwest. He pulled out the seats and fitted the inside of the bus with hand-built wooden furnishings, cleverly designed so that everything could be turned into some-thing else: the table they ate their meals on and she and her older brother, Gus, did their homework on became the base for the futon her parents rolled out each night. She and Gus slept in berths—hers was on the bottom—and Susan had sewed bedspreads into curtains that could be drawn for privacy. Each of them had a handsome wooden trunk for personal belongings. The trunks had pillows on top so they could be used as seats.

The bus kitchen was like a playhouse, with its tiny sink, stove, and refrigerator. Somebody had to shop for groceries every day since there was no space to store much food, except sacks of pinto beans stowed on top of the bus and *ristras* of red chiles that hung along the side, drying in the sun. One thing they did have space for was books. April's father studied philosophy and astronomy as well as all kinds of crafts.

Susan waited tables at a natural foods res-taurant, and Tom worked for a landscape company. They grew a lot of their own food.

It had taken them a while to get used to New Mexico's dry climate, but the property where they parked their bus had water rights. On certain days each month, when it was their turn, Tom opened the sluice gate from the *acequias,* the irrigation ditches that crisscrossed the river valley, and let the water run into the small ditch that ran through their property. Their garden thrived. Now they had rows of corn, a chile patch, and all the fresh tomatoes and zucchini and beans they could eat. Good thing they were vegetarians.

Last winter Tom had decided it was time to build them a house. He brought home piles of books from the library and pored over them every night while April and her brother did homework.

"It's going to be adobe," her father said. "Basically, dried mud. We'll make the adobes ourselves, just like the early settlers did and lots of folks still do today in some parts of New Mexico."

Her mother glanced up from the turquoise beads she was stringing. "Sounds like a lot of hard work," she said.

"Yes, but it's simple," Tom insisted. "This book tells you exactly how to do it. And since we've got the clay right here on our land, why go out and buy materials?"

On the first warm spring day, Tom built wooden forms like a series of shallow boxes to make the large, flat, adobe bricks, which would be several times bigger than ordinary fired bricks. Gus began spading up the dirt in one corner of the lot. Then April and Susan opened the gate of the *acequia*. They all helped mix the dirt and the ditchwater to make a thick, gooey mud, tromping around in it in their bare feet. After lunch that first day it turned into a mud fight when Gus tossed the first handful. All four of them got completely covered and had to run down to the main channel to rinse themselves off. Then they got back to work seriously again.

Tom shoveled the mud into the wooden forms, which were laid flat on the ground, open on the bottom to allow the excess water to drain away. The Ellises could make a dozen adobes at a time, letting one batch set while they shoveled mud into another form. "More mud!" Tom would yell, and Gus would rush up with another wheelbarrowful. April tried to run the wheelbarrow, but she had no idea mud could be so heavy. When the adobe bricks had dried out enough to handle, Susan and April stood them on edge, lined up like dominoes to finish drying.

At the end of the day they were all so sore and tired they could hardly move. But they forgot to cover the finished adobes, and when a rainstorm came up suddenly during the night, the adobes melted right back to mud again. Then, because the clay was so dense and Tom hadn't mixed in enough straw, their next batch cracked.

If it hadn't been for one of their neighbors, old Mr. Flores, they might not have gotten anywhere. Tom read his books faithfully, but Mr. Flores had actually built his own adobe house when he was a young man. He came over when he saw them out working and stood around smoking his pipe and offering bits of advice. "Good to wet your forms before you shovel in the mud," he said. "Adobes come out easier." He also showed Tom how to tell if the adobes were ready to use: he broke one in half so they could see that it was still dark in the center, not quite dry enough yet.

April noticed, though, that Mr. Flores himself lived in an ordinary house with fake stone decorating the front and aluminum windows and a concrete patio painted brick color.

He sure wasn't living in any adobe house now. And once she heard him say to another neighbor who had stopped by to watch, "You'd think he'd buy his adobes, no? The kind with stabilizer mixed in, so his house won't melt around him!"

Every evening and all day Saturday and Sunday April's family mixed mud and made adobes. By the end of July there were several stacks of bricks protected by sheets of tarpaper, enough to start building the house.

Tom insisted on making their home authentic. The traditional flat roof would be supported by *vigas,* beams made of peeled pine logs, which April was afraid, knowing her dad, he'd want to chop down himself in the forest. She was relieved when he mentioned that he had ordered the *vigas* from a man in Española, as well as the *latillas,* thin cottonwood saplings to be laid across the beams.

In the old days, Tom told them, adobe walls were laid right on the ground, but Mr. Flores convinced him the building inspector wouldn't allow it. Better to set them on concrete that would keep the adobes from soaking up groundwater. But Tom clung stubbornly to the idea of an earthen floor—somewhere he'd read about mixing the dirt with animal blood to make it hard and shiny. The idea made April sick.

She knew that some of her friends had rooms of their own where they could keep stuffed animals on the bed and put up posters all over the walls, if they wanted to, and could invite friends to sleep over. But as long as she lived in an old bus with her parents sleeping on the table on the other side of the curtain and her brother in his berth only inches above her head, there was no way she'd invite a friend to spend the night.

When the house was finished, she thought, then she could have someone visit. But when April took a good look at the floor plan Tom had been fussing over, her dream evaporated. The house seemed to be just one big room. "Where's my room?" she asked.

"That's it," he said. "The main room is your room and everybody's room, just like in the old days. Everybody cooked and ate and bathed and slept in that one room. For the first couple of years, that's how we'll do it. See the fireplace over here in the corner? That's probably all we'll need for heat. Adobe is much more energy-efficient than some people believe," he continued, explaining why they'd have just small windows and whitewash on the walls and so on. He seemed to have forgotten about April's wish for a room of her own. "You're going to love it, April! Maybe in a couple of years when we've saved up some more money and made some more adobes, we can build extra rooms onto it."

A couple of years! She'd be grown-up and gone by the time her father got around to adding a room for her!

The first part of the house was still far from finished, no more than an outline of the big room and part of two walls when Nana and Poppy came out from Philadelphia to visit over Labor Day weekend, driving over from the motel in their rental car to stare disapprovingly at the piles of mud-colored bricks.

"How can you live like this, Thomas?" Poppy had asked sadly, and April felt sorry for her father. Actually the yard looked kind of like the ancient Indian ruins they had gone to visit. Wild purple asters bloomed in the field, and strings of bright red chiles were turning dark on the side of the bus.

Later Mr. Flores began to tease her. "And are you going to be the *enjarradora*, April?" he asked.

She didn't understand what he meant. Susan studied with Spanish language tapes, and

April was supposed to be learning, too, but she could say no more than a couple of polite phrases. She couldn't even pronounce the word he had just used. "What?"

"In our tradition, it's the women who plaster the adobe," he explained. "*Enjarrar* means 'to plaster.' *La enjarradora* is 'the woman who plasters.' She puts it on with her hands, like this," and he pretended to pat mud on her head.

"Not me," she said, ducking away and hoping her father hadn't heard about that authentic custom.

So far nobody at Rio Grande School knew about the bus or the adobe house or about her hippie parents, and April was completely thrown the fourth week of school by Mr. Wilder's announcement to the Heritage Project. "April's father has volunteered to come next week and help us build an *horno*," he said. "Anybody know what that is?"

Tomás Jaramillo raised his hand. "It's an outdoor oven."

"That's right. You see a lot of them around here."

Pauline Romero spoke up. "We have them at the pueblo," she said. "We bake bread in them. And also dry corn."

"And that's what we'll do with ours, once we get it built," Mr. Wilder said. "Be sure to bring old clothes because we're going to be covered with mud before it's over. I understand Mr. Ellis is building his own adobe house—is that correct, April?"

She was barely able to nod. Her tongue seemed to be cemented to the roof of her mouth. Tom had not said a word about this offer. Was it his idea of a joke? What made him *do* such a thing and without even discussing it with her first! She was so angry she was close to tears.

That evening at supper, while they ate their usual squash and chile and pinto beans, April burst out, "Why didn't you tell me you were going to volunteer? At least ask me! I was so embarrassed!"

Her father looked at her with innocent blue eyes. "I thought it would be a nice surprise, that's all," he said mildly. "I'm sorry if it upset you, but I'm not sure why you're embarrassed that I offered to come in to share a skill with your class."

"Your skill!" April yelped. "Tom, you don't even know how to build an *horno*. You've never built one before in your whole entire life!"

He seemed utterly amazed. "Just because I've never actually built one doesn't mean I can't learn. I'll be learning right along with your class. That's what education's all about, isn't it?"

All week April kept hoping it wouldn't happen. After all, her father was notorious in the family for not getting around to doing things he had promised to do. But on Friday morning he offered to drive her to school. The old wheelbarrow and some lumber and a couple of shovels were in the back of the truck. Climbing into the passenger seat, April could not see how she'd survive this day.

April walked into the school pretending that the tall, thin man in mud-spattered overalls, his long hair flowing out from beneath a red bandanna, was a complete stranger. Her strategy didn't work. Everyone stared. But then Mr. Wilder introduced him—just as "Mr. Ellis" and not as "April's father"—and Tom began to talk about the history of adobe making. After the first few minutes the kids seemed to accept Tom for what he was—an interesting man.

"Did you know that the *horno* originated in the Middle East maybe a thousand years ago? The Moors introduced it to Spain in the

Middle Ages, and the Spanish brought it to the New World."

After the history lesson they went outside, and Mrs. Salazar, the principal, came along to help pick the place they were going to build the *horno*. The custodian brought out two more shovels, and everybody took turns spading up the earth. Since the school wasn't on an *acequia,* they ran a couple of lengths of hose out from the outdoor faucet, and everybody waded around in the gooey mud. April, who had done it lots of times at home, showed them how.

Several kids built the forms, sawing and nailing the lumber under Tom's guidance. They took turns with the wheelbarrow, dumping mud into the forms. Soon they had a long line of adobes drying in the sun.

"That's all for today," Tom announced, squinting at the sky. "They'll dry over the weekend. Monday we build the *horno*."

It hadn't been as bad as April expected. She didn't hesitate when her father offered her a ride to school on Monday.

The Heritage Project kids were eager to get on with the next step. Tom directed them to lay out a circular bed of flat stones about three and a half feet across and to arrange a layer of adobes on top of the stones. Manuel

97

Medina put himself in charge of hauling the mud that would go around and between and over this base. Next they set a circle of adobes on edge, cementing them together with mud, then added another row on top of that one. "More mud!" somebody would yell, and Manuel would stagger over with the loaded wheelbarrow.

Tom helped them form the arched opening to the oven and showed them where to put the smoke hole on the north side. They began to tilt the rows inward, gradually forming the beehive shape. They chinked the spaces between the adobes with mud.

It looked great, everyone agreed. "One more step," Mr. Ellis announced, taking off his bandanna and wiping mud out of his beard.

"Enjarrar," April said, surprised that she could remember Mr. Flores's word. "That means 'to plaster.' It's the women's job, putting on the smooth finish." She looked around at the girls in the class. "We're the *enjarradoras,"* she explained. "It's very messy work—the same adobe mud, only more runny. It's up to us to make it look good. Will you guys stand back, *por favor?"*

The girls looked at each other. "All *right!"* said Jacquelyn Cox. "Let's get going."

"More mud!" April called out, and Manuel ran toward their mixing hole with the wheelbarrow.

When they had finished, they had mud everywhere—on their clothes, their shoes, their arms, their faces. The Heritage Project kids clustered around Tom, asking when they could build a fire in their *horno* and bake some bread or roast some chiles. They could fire it up anytime, he told them.

"Pretty soon," April said when they were cleaning up their tools, "you can all come up and see the house we're building. It's an authentic adobe. Actually," she added, "the bus we're living in is really neat, too."

CHILE—RED OR GREEN?

❊

by April Ellis

WHENEVER *you order New Mexican food in a restaurant, the waitress always asks, "Red or green?" She means, Which kind of chile do you want on your enchilada? Or your burrito or stuffed sopaipilla or huevos rancheros, or whatever you ordered. In my family my mother always orders green, my brother and I order red, and my father says, "Navidad," the word for Christmas, which means he wants some of both, red and green.*

Some people ask, "Which is hotter?" The answer is, they can both be pretty hot. Just ask my grandparents from Philadelphia, who won't touch the stuff. Or they can be fairly mild. There are lots of different kinds of chiles, and some kinds are hotter than others. Red is not necessarily any hotter than green. Red chile has just had a chance to ripen.

The chile is the state vegetable of New Mexico. Chile has been grown in the Rio Grande valley for at least four hundred years. The Aztec Indians used to grow it in Mexico. Chile is the Spanish word

*for it, but some people spell it c-h-i-l-i. The scientific
name for it is* Capsicum. *When you cut open a
chile, you will find seeds and veins inside. There is
a chemical in the veins called capsaicin, and that's
what makes it hot. This chemical is so strong that
in its pure form your taste buds can detect it even
when it is diluted to one part in a million.*

*Most chile is grown commercially in the south-
ern part of the state, but around here lots of people
grow enough for themselves. We have some in our
garden. We have been eating it since the middle of
July, and my mother says we can keep on picking
it until frost. Chile is good for you. It has a lot of
Vitamin A and Vitamin C—more than in an orange. The later in the season you pick it, the more
vitamins it has stored.*

*Also, chile makes you sweat, which cools you
off. That's why people in hot countries eat spicy
food. If it tastes too hot and burns your mouth,
DON'T DRINK WATER. Instead, eat something
sweet, like honey, or drink a little milk to put out
the fire. I don't know why, but it works.*

Green chiles must be roasted in an horno *or
some kind of oven to loosen the tough skins. It's a
good idea to wear gloves when you peel the chiles,
and be careful not to get any in your eyes.*

*We eat green chiles from our garden in the
summer. When they turn red in September, my*

mother knots them into long strings called ristras, which she hangs in the sun to dry so they won't spoil, and we have red chile to eat all winter. Red chiles don't need to be roasted and skinned. You grind up the whole thing.

Here are some of my mother's recipes using red and green chiles. The measurements are not exact because it depends how much cheese and onions and chile you like.

HUEVOS RANCHEROS, RED

Wash about a dozen dried red chile pods, open them, and take out some of the seeds and veins, and soak the pods in hot water for an hour. Put them in a blender a few at a time with some of the water and grind them up very fine. Blend in a clove of garlic and a little salt. Then cook this sauce for a few minutes over low heat. Be careful not to let it burn.

Start with two corn tortillas. (My mother makes her own, but you can buy them at the supermarket.) Heat some oil in a frying pan and dip each tortilla in the oil for a few seconds. Put two hot tortillas on a plate and cover them with a layer of cooked pinto beans. Put a fried egg on top of the beans and pour some cooked red chile over it. Sprinkle grated yellow cheese on top and put the plate in a warm oven long enough to melt the cheese.

CHEESE ENCHILADAS, GREEN

Peel the skins off some roasted green chiles and take out most of the veins and seeds. (You can also buy them frozen or canned.) Chop up the chiles. Fry a clove of garlic chopped fine and a small chopped raw onion in a little oil. Add the chiles and a little water and cook them for about five minutes. (Some people add a little flour to thicken the sauce, but my mother doesn't.)

For each enchilada you need three corn tortillas plus about half a cup of grated yellow cheese and a little raw onion chopped fine. Heat some oil in a frying pan and dip each tortilla in the oil for a few seconds. Put the tortilla on a plate, pour green chile sauce over it, and sprinkle it with cheese and onion. That's the first layer. Add two more layers, ending with cheese. Put it in a warm oven to melt the cheese.

CALABACITAS
"Little Squashes"

Fry some chopped onion and chopped garlic in a little oil. Slice three medium-size zucchini or yellow squash and add it to the onion and garlic. Add a cup of corn (canned or frozen or fresh) and half a cup of chopped green chile, plus some salt. Cook until the squash is soft. Sprinkle in about a cup of grated yellow cheese and cover with a lid until the cheese melts.

P.S. Mr. Flores told me a story about calabaza, *which is Spanish for squash. He said in the old days when a girl didn't want to accept a boy's proposal of marriage, she'd leave a big squash on his doorstep.*

TOMÁS JARAMILLO

✺

Another Española Joke

Did you hear about the tornado that touched down in Española and did three million dollars' worth of improvements?

Tomás Jaramillo remembered this joke as he and his family drove through Española, a small town eighty-five miles up river from Albuquerque, on their way to a christening. *How come,* Tomás wondered, *of all the towns in New Mexico, Española always gets picked on for jokes?* It didn't seem fair.

There were so many jokes about the place that even the mayor of Española got mad. The mayor went to the state legislature and asked them please not to make those jokes about his town, which was really such a great place. The jokes made people from Española sound poor and stupid, but mostly stupid.

Question: Why did they cancel the driver education course at Española High School?
Answer: The burro died.

Tomás had been born in Española, and he lived there until his parents moved to the city when he was in third grade. He didn't let on to the other kids in Albuquerque that he was from Española because they might have teased him, calling him a *cholo,* a "punk."

Question: Who discovered Española?
Answer: Marco Cholo.

Going back there wasn't easy, either. His *primos,* his cousins, always teased him about being from *río abajo,* the lower river, which is what they called the Rio Grande below Santa Fe.

"A city kid from Albuquerque," they said, snickering, and they used a lot of Spanish slang that he didn't understand to remind him he was an outsider, even if he was their cousin. He was the youngest and always seemed to get the worst of it. Once he decided to try out a joke he had heard. He asked his cousin Benny, who was older than Tomás but short, like all of his Española cousins, "You know why they're taking out all the drive-in windows in Española?"

"They taking them out?" Benny asked innocently, not realizing it was a joke.

"Sure they are," Tomás said, trying to keep a straight face. "Taking 'em out of the banks, the Dairy Queen, everywhere." He couldn't believe Benny was walking right into this.

"Well, why?"

"Because the windows are too high! Get it? Because everybody's so short!" And Tomás started laughing so hard he didn't even see Benny's fist coming at him until it was too late and he ended up with a bloody nose.

Tomás' father and his uncles always laughed at Española jokes, but his mother and his aunt who were born in Española didn't think they were funny at all. They pinched their mouths shut tight, and angry looks flew from their eyes. Who were the Jaramillos to talk, his mother demanded? Being from Tierra Amarilla in northern Rio Arriba County where people were well known to do

really crazy things, she told his father, the Jaramillos had no room to poke fun at Española
in the southern part of the county.

It really *didn't* seem fair. Española was a
great place, Tomás thought, and he loved to
go there to see the low riders and visit all his
relatives, even if they did tease him.

Some of the cousins who used to give him
a hard time were grown-up and married and
even had little kids of their own. In fact one
of these kids—Eduardo, Carlota and Enrique's baby—was being baptized in Santa
Cruz Church, which is why Tomás was all
dressed up in a white shirt and a necktie that
was choking him.

After mass the whole family and many
friends were invited to the baby's grandparents' house for a big feast. The main course
was to be *cabrito,* roasted young goat. Enrique
and some of the baby's uncles had dug a pit,
built a fire in it long before sunrise, and buried
the meat in the glowing embers with a thick
layer of dirt on top. They left the goat to roast
slowly while they were at church. Friends and
neighbors brought platters and casseroles,
everything from tamales to potato salad, and
there was a beautiful cake and bowls of fluffy
natillas for dessert.

But it wasn't the food that grabbed Tomás' attention. So many of the guests came in low-slung, elaborately decorated cars that it was like a low-rider show right there in the front yard of Carlota's father's home. Among the last to arrive, timed for a grand entrance, was the baby's godfather, Johnny Aragón, who drove up in his 1980 Cadillac Seville that had been gorgeously customized from bumper to bumper. Johnny was another *primo*.

Soon all the men and a lot of the women were standing around outside, paying more attention to the beautiful cars than they were to the guest of honor, baby Eduardo. In Tomás' opinion, Johnny Aragón's Caddy, which he had named *Mi Güisa*—My Sweetheart— was definitely the best low rider showing off at the party.

The Cadillac was painted dark, lustrous red with gold metal flecks that shimmered richly in the sunlight. Sinuous orange and pink ribbons were painted along the sides of the car, looping and swirling from the chrome hood ornament to the tips of the rear fenders. The interior was lushly upholstered in thick black crushed velvet—seats, doors, floor, dash, everything, even the trunk. A small statue of the Virgin stood on the dashboard. And the steering wheel, only six inches across, was made of chain links that had been welded and chrome-plated.

Question: Why do low riders have those tiny steering wheels?
Answer: So they can steer with their handcuffs on.

But the most unusual thing about the car was the painting on the enormous hood: a nearly life-size portrait of the Virgin of Guadalupe, surrounded by her blue-and-gold circle of light. Her hands were outstretched toward the Santuario de Chimayó—the old church in a nearby village—that lay spread out at her feet. It was so realistic that it looked like a photograph. Johnny leaned against the door, answering questions and accepting compliments from admirers.

Tomás hovered around, listening to the car owners talk. His grandfather came over and wrapped an arm around Tomás' shoulders. "In my day," he said, "we had hot rods and dragsters. They were built for speed, not for beauty. We thought we were hot stuff! But that was a long time ago. Today people just like to cruise around. They're not in any hurry to get anywhere, 'cause there's nowhere to go. The young guys go cruising on Friday and Saturday nights with their dates, radios blasting your ears off, but Sunday, that's family day. You cruise to show off your car, your prized possession. If I had the money, man . . ."

Tomás knew his grandmother didn't think much of the whole idea. "Huh," she said to Johnny, "it seems pretty foolish when you've got a wife and child and you're living in a rented double-wide in a trailer park, and you spend all your money on a *car*." Tomás couldn't believe she'd say this to Johnny.

But Johnny took her criticism good-humoredly. "It's more than a car, Abuelita," he explained. "It's my life. It's who I am, I guess you could say."

"Huh," Grandmother snorted.

As the afternoon passed and everyone had had enough to eat, the guests got into their cars and drove away, taking care not to scrape the undercarriages that cleared the ground by only a couple of inches. Tomás had been thinking of going inside to see if there was any cake and *natillas* left, but he couldn't seem to tear himself away as long as any of the beautiful cars were still parked along the side of the road and up on the flower-edged lawn.

"Want to go cruising?"

It was Johnny, grinning at him, holding open the door of *Mi Güisa*.

Tomás glanced around and saw his mother with the crying baby Eduardo on her shoulder, jiggling him and patting his back. They wouldn't be starting back to Albuquerque any time soon. "You bet!" he told his cousin.

Johnny slid behind the chain-link steering wheel. His wife, Catalina, sat next to him, and two-year-old Arturo was already strapped into his car seat padded with the same black velvet. Tomás climbed in next to Arturo and nestled against the deep upholstery, tucked and stitched to form velvety diamonds. It was like a cave inside the car. There was even a tiny TV built into a console beside him.

"Catalina's on the button," Johnny said to him in the rearview mirror.

"On the button?"

"You'll see."

With exquisite care, Johnny guided the car out of the yard and headed west toward the main street of Española. The narrow two-lane road was already backed up with a line of cars waiting to get through the light. While they inched along, Johnny explained that his father had done most of the work on the interior and all of the bodywork himself.

"First the base coat, then a few coats of metal-flake paint, and then I don't know how many coats of the brick-red candy. Those translucent candy coats are what make it deep and shimmery, like you're looking down into a pool of water. Some ways you look at it it's red, and other ways it looks black. An artist from Santa Fe airbrushed those ribbons on the sides. I helped install the suspension system. Those hydraulic pumps are powered by five batteries. Watch."

Pressing the button, Catalina demonstrated how alternating the pumps made the car "hop" up and down, and the little boy in the car seat chuckled happily. Johnny's father had given the car to Johnny and Catalina for a wedding present three years ago and then turned right around and bought himself another car to work on. "I'm helping him restore it," Johnny told Tomás. "It'll take years."

When Arturo was born, the proud grandfather presented Johnny and Catalina with a miniature of *Mi Güisa:* a little car, the kind you pedal, decorated exactly to match

Johnny's, right down to the black velvet upholstery and the airbrushed ribbons.

Then for Johnny's birthday—he turned twenty-five in August—Catalina and her parents and Johnny's parents all chipped in to have the painting of the Virgin of Guadalupe done on the hood. It was even signed and dated by the artist. Catalina said proudly, "He was so pleased he almost broke down and cried."

"No way," Johnny protested, but Tomás suspected she was telling the truth.

Once they got through the light and out onto Riverside, Johnny joined another long line at the carwash. While they waited their turn, Johnny told Tomás how much everything cost, counting it off on his fingers.

"First you buy the car," he explained. "Then you start fixing it up. Maybe thirteen hundred for the hydro. About thirty-five hundred for the exterior paint job, including the flared fenders with the antennae built into them, plus thirty-five for the interior. The customized wheels set me back twelve hundred. The grill with chrome bumpers, add about fifteen hundred. If you chrome the underbody, another maybe fifteen hundred. My dad did most of it himself, but if you get it done in the shops around town, it adds up."

Tomás, who was good at math, had been adding in his head, and he came up with a total of twelve thousand five hundred dollars. "Not counting the birthday present," Johnny said with a grin. "They won't tell me what that cost. And, of course, not counting the car."

When it was their turn, Johnny tenderly bathed and polished *Mi Güisa* while Catalina vacuumed the floor and wiped the inside of the windows. "I change the oil every Monday morning before I go to work," Johnny said. "That engine is as clean on the inside as it is on the outside."

When Johnny was satisfied that *Mi Güisa* was perfect, they joined the procession down Riverside. Dozens and dozens of cars, all of them chromed and painted and decorated and now washed and polished, started at Sonic North, the drive-in restaurant at the north end of the strip, and crept slowly, five miles an hour max, south through Española, past the gas stations and the fast-food places and Big Rock Shopping Center, on down to Sonic South, where they turned around and headed north again.

Question: What's the Low Rider 500?
**Answer: Last one to creep across the finish
line wins.**

Some teenagers showed off in cheapy little
cars and trucks painted intense bubblegum
colors, their neon-bright windshield wipers
angled out from the window and waving back
and forth, back and forth. But everyone
understood that those cars were just toys, kid
stuff. The real dream car was the old car made
newer than new, better than it had ever been,
transformed into a work of art.

Tomás leaned back against the velvety
seat. *This,* he decided, *is pure heaven.* Someday
he would have one of these cars. He could
picture himself slouched carelessly, as Johnny
was, behind a chain-link steering wheel. *Someday.* But for right now, the thing that would
make him happiest was if the kids in his Heritage Project class could somehow get to see
this incredible car.

Dreamily Tomás asked, "D'you think you
could bring *Mi Güisa* to my school sometime?"

"Albuquerque's a long way from here."

"Not really. You'd drive it faster if you
raised it up, no? Only maybe an hour and a
half."

"I'd have to think about it."

At least Johnny hadn't said no.

. . .

A few weeks later on a perfect fall day when the sky was deep blue and the dry air was still, Mrs. Salazar came to Tomás' classroom. Tomás blinked: Johnny was with her. "You have a visitor," the principal said and introduced Johnny to Mr. Wilder. "This is Mr. Aragón. He has a special surprise for you. I'll let him explain it, Mr. Wilder."

Tomás stood up at his desk and leaned forward. "Johnny," he said.

"Hey, Tomás! Sorry I didn't have a chance to call first. I just found out I had to make a trip down." He winked at Tomás. "Guess what I got outside?"

"Mi Güisa?"

"Sí."

"This is my *primo,* my cousin," Tomás announced to the class. "He's got a low rider."

Tomás heard some giggles behind him. He knew what some of them thought when they heard "low rider": another Española joke. "Can we go outside for just a minute and look?" Tomás pleaded.

Permission granted, the students rushed

out of the classroom and around to the front of the building. There sat *Mi Güisa,* resplendent in the morning sunlight. For a moment they stared at the car, awestruck, and then walked slowly toward it.

"Don't touch it!" Tomás yelled, but Johnny laid a hand on Tomás' shoulder.

"It's all right," he said. "They won't hurt it. Fingerprints will come off."

In a moment the four doors, the hood, and the trunk all stood open while the kids gawked at the tiny steering wheel, the immaculately chromed engine, the beautiful painting of the Virgin and the church. They examined every detail, right down to the red plastic dice that Johnny used to replace the valve caps on the tires and Tomás hadn't even noticed before.

"There are some things you ought to know about low riders," Johnny told the class. "The whole low rider thing started back in the sixties with the *cholos* out in East L.A., and then somehow the idea got to Chimayó and Española."

Tomás stood back proudly while they examined everything and asked questions, which Johnny answered carefully. He even explained that the chain-link steering wheel represented Jesus' crown of thorns.

And he told them about the low rider that had gone to Washington, D.C.

"There was this guy named David Jaramillo, no relation to Tomás' family, who once owned a 1969 Ford LTD that was his pride and joy. He spent all his spare time and money on that car. His dream was to win the biggest low-rider show in East L.A. But he got killed in an accident before he finished it, and his relatives put the car in storage.

"Then one day some guy came around and said he wanted to buy the car to put in the Smithsonian in Washington. So they got the car out of storage and started working on it so it would be good enough to be in the museum. I belong to the low-rider club that worked on the car. We wanted it to be perfect. Seventy-five people had a hand in it," he said. "The priest came and blessed it before it got shipped to Washington. Someday I'm going there to see it. It's called Dave's Dream."

Then Johnny offered to take them for a short ride around the school's circular driveway to show them how the hydraulic system worked. "You pick who's to go first," he said to Tomás, and Tomás chose Franklyn, because he wasn't from around here, and Manuel, the Mexican kid, because he was having such a tough time with his English, and Sara, to show he had nothing against girls. Those three scrambled into the backseat, big grins on their faces, and Tomás sat in the passenger seat so that he could press the button to activate the hydraulic system.

Johnny drove the car at the stately pace of five miles an hour while Tomás made it hop. He saw faces peering out of the other classrooms, staring at them. This had to be the best day of his whole life.

Watching the next group climb into the backseat, Tomás remembered one more Española joke:

This guy's taking a bunch of penguins from a zoo somewhere up north to the Albuquerque Zoo and his truck breaks down in Española and it's too late to get it fixed. Then a low rider comes by in his big car with the chain-link steering wheel and offers to help out. The truck driver is real grateful and asks the low rider if he'll take the penguins to the zoo and gives the guy some money. So all the penguins are put in the low rider's velvet-lined car, and they take off.

The next day the truck driver picks up his truck at the garage, and he can't believe his eyes: here comes the low rider with all the penguins sitting in the backseat.

"Hey, I thought I told you to take those penguins to the zoo!" says the truck driver.

"I did, man," says the low rider, "I took 'em to the zoo, I took 'em to the tram, I took 'em all over town! They had a great time, man!"

Even Mr. Wilder had a ride, and then Ricky Begay set up his camera with the shutter on a timer and took a picture of the car with all the Heritage Project students clustered around it.

"We'll put the picture in our book," Jeremy Steinberg said as they watched Johnny and *Mi Güisa* drive away.

"That can be your contribution, Tomás," added Rosa Gonzales, the literary editor.

Tomás smiled. "We'll call it *Española Joke*," he said, and knew that nobody would dare to laugh at this one.

FRANKLYN AND
JACQUELYN COX

❈

Thanksgiving Stranger

MOST of the guests had already arrived for the Coxes' annual Thanksgiving potluck dinner when Jacquelyn Cox strode in wearing a stark black suit with sleeves that hung down past her thumbs, heavy black stockings, her hair wrapped in a white scarf, and a black hat with a wide brim set on top of that. Jacquie, who loved to parade around in weird costumes, acted like she didn't notice everybody staring at her, but her brother, Franklyn, knew she gloried in the attention.

"You all dressed up like a Pilgrim, honey?" asked Mrs. Bishop, a teacher at Mrs. Cox's school. Mrs. Bishop, who came from

Louisiana, set a big pot of gumbo on the stove.

Jacquie did look a little like a Pilgrim, Franklyn thought, except that white scarf under the broad-brimmed hat wasn't Pilgrimish.

"I'm Georgia O'Keeffe," Jacquelyn announced gravely.

"Georgia O'Keeffe! That lady artist who painted all the cow skulls?" asked a neighbor, Mrs. Burkhardt, on her way into the kitchen with a pie in each hand.

"Yes, ma'am," Jacquie said, now all smiles.

"Is one permitted to ask *why* you're dressed up like Georgia O'Keeffe?" asked Major Cox, their father.

"Because I'm writing about her life for the Heritage Project book at our school," Jacquie explained, basking in the limelight, "and I want to feel what it's like to walk in her shoes—"

"But she's about a hundred years old, isn't she?" Franklyn blurted out.

Jacquelyn gazed at him coolly. "She's dead, Franklyn. She died in 1986 at the age of ninety-eight. But this is how she dressed when she was alive. The other reason I'm dressed this way, if you don't mind not interrupting me, Frankie, is that I intend to be as famous someday as Georgia O'Keeffe. I'm going to be an artist when I grow up."

"Oh, man," Franklyn muttered under his breath.

"That's what she says this week," Franklyn's mother murmured. "Next week it'll be something else."

True, Franklyn thought. But at least she was out of her African princess phase, during which she was convinced she was descended from the black queen of some African country. Franklyn himself thought that was a stupid idea. If it made Jacquie feel good, all right, but generally she just used that black queen stuff as an excuse for bossing him around. Franklyn had no idea who *he* was descended from, although since he was Jacquie's twin brother it had to have been from the same royal line, which made him a prince, didn't it? He really didn't care much. Royalty was the kind of thing girls liked.

"Doesn't matter so much what you come from as what you're going to be," his father always said. His father was a major in the Air Force, a pilot who flew huge planes. Franklyn wished he knew what he was going to be, but so far he didn't have a clue.

"Well, I *am* going to be an artist," Jacquie informed their Thanksgiving guests. "Someday I'll be known as the black Georgia O'Keeffe."

"What's wrong with being known as Jacquelyn Cox?" Major Cox wanted to know.

"Nothing. That's after I'm famous and have a beautiful house in Santa Fe and my work is being sold in galleries and shown in museums. But comparisons are inevitable, Dad."

Give me a break, thought Franklyn.

"She hasn't been the same since she discovered Santa Fe," Mrs. Cox explained with a chuckle.

"I love the adobe houses," Jacquie said. "The subtle earth tones." She wasn't laughing. She was dead serious.

Franklyn wished Jacquelyn had not brought up the subject of the Heritage Project. It reminded him—and he did not want to be reminded—that he still didn't know what he was going to write about for their book. Jeremy Steinberg had asked him a couple of days ago how his article was going.

"Fine," Franklyn had said, although he didn't have the faintest idea what he would do for the project. "I'm working on the research."

"Are you going to write about African Americans in New Mexico?" Jeremy prodded.

"Wait and see," Franklyn replied with what he hoped was a mysterious smile. It was still a total mystery to him.

Jacquelyn kept on talking about Georgia O'Keeffe and Santa Fe in that sohisticated way that drove him crazy. Franklyn knew it was better to ignore her when she got like this, but Jacquie was hard to ignore. In Franklyn's opinion twins didn't necessarily have any more in common than any other two members of the same family.

The last thing in the world Franklyn wanted was for people to notice him. His mother was all dressed up for the holiday in her beautiful *kinte* cloth dress, and she wore lots of jewelry, shell necklaces draped around her neck, a wristful of jangling brass bracelets. His father, of course, dressed as conservatively as usual. Even in a plaid shirt and blue slacks, the major managed to look military. Franklyn hated getting dressed up.

This was their third Thanksgiving in New Mexico. Before that it had been Florida, and before that Virginia. Wherever their father was stationed, their mother always rounded up people who were far away from their homes and families for Thanksgiving and organized a potluck. She'd invite everybody to come over to their place and bring some food to share, some childhood favorite. But if somebody couldn't bring anything, that was all right, too—there was more than enough to go around. Mrs. Cox always roasted a big turkey with cornbread stuffing, but that was the only dependable item on the menu. You never could be sure what you'd end up with. One year they had about six kinds of potatoes and no cranberry sauce, but nobody seemed to mind.

People had begun arriving around noon, carrying their casseroles and pans, and as always the men drifted toward the TV to watch football while the women gathered in the cramped little kitchen. It was Jacquelyn and Franklyn's job to play with the visiting kids, distracting them until it was time to eat to keep them from swooping into the kitchen and getting underfoot.

Jacquie snagged a little boy who was yanking on a corner of the tablecloth. He turned and lunged for her black hat and then started to howl when she wouldn't let him have it.

"How come you're writing about Georgia O'Keeffe for the Heritage Project book?" Franklyn asked her. "I thought we're supposed to write about our own heritage."

"Georgia O'Keeffe *is* part of my heritage," Jacquie said, trying to calm the little boy. "*A,* she was a great artist. *B,* she was a woman. And *C,* she lived in New Mexico although she came from someplace else originally. Everybody associates her with New Mexico. In fact, I'll bet you anything she's the most famous artist in New Mexico."

"But she's not black."

"Well, of course she's not, Frankie! So what?"

Franklyn couldn't think of an answer. Maybe his sister was right. Maybe that wasn't so important. He grabbed the little boy who had turned to pulling the leaves off one of his mother's houseplants. He wished the kid's mother would come and rescue him, but he didn't know which one was his mother.

As usual, Franklyn didn't recognize a lot of the people who were crowded into their small house near the Air Force base. He wasn't sure where his mother found them all each year. Some were usually from whatever school she was teaching at. Others, he couldn't imagine where she met them.

This year Franklyn had been with her when she invited a homeless family standing on the corner of Rio Grande and Central, holding up a sign that said: HOMELESS—WILL WORK FOR FOOD. Mrs. Cox stopped the car and leaned out. "We'll talk about work later," she said. "Right now it's Thanksgiving. Just come." She gave them her address and bus fare.

Now the couple waited near the door, looking around nervously and holding tightly to a couple of little girls with pale blond hair. Mrs. Cox sailed in from the kitchen and introduced them: "This is Bob and Marty Adams and their children. What are your names, girls?" She bent down to hear their whispered reply. "Sharon and Robbie," she repeated. Mrs. Bishop went over to talk to them and when she found out they were from Louisiana too, they finally started to relax.

At last the bowls and platters of food were set out on the dining-room table; the pies were kept in the kitchen for later. Mrs. Cox, who was a member of the church choir, got everybody singing "Praise God from Whom All Blessings Flow." They were harmonizing on the "Amen" when the doorbell rang again.

Franklyn opened the door for an old black man, white haired and stooped, with a face as lined and wrinkled as a crumpled paper sack. His baggy pants were cinched around his skinny waist with a worn-out belt, and he felt his way into the room with a cane. He carried a little jar in one trembling hand.

"I brought some grape jelly," he said, holding out the jar to whoever would take it.

Mrs. Cox guided him to a chair. "Why, I surely do thank you. You come right in and make yourself at home. Franklyn's going to fix you up a plate."

"Yes, ma'am," said the old man. "I'm grateful to you."

"Who's the old guy?" Jacquie whispered as Franklyn made the rounds of the steaming casseroles, putting a spoonful of this, a dab of that on a plate. Franklyn noticed that his sister had managed to extract most of the baby marshmallows from the sweet potato casserole and had arranged them on her own plate.

Franklyn shrugged. "Somebody Mom knows, I guess."

Franklyn took the heaping plate to the old man and went back to help himself to some food. There weren't enough chairs, even though the Burkhardts had brought over some extras. Most people found a space on the floor and sat down cross-legged, balancing their plates on their knees. Franklyn found a spot next to Mrs. Adams.

"Hi," she said. "Good food, huh?"

"It's always good," Franklyn said. "People bring great stuff." Then he wished he hadn't said that because she hadn't brought anything. He looked at the little girls who sat primly beside their mother. "Are they twins?"

"Yeah. You and your sister are twins, right? I should ask your advice. What's it like, being a twin?"

"It's okay," he said, watching Georgia O'Keeffe dabbing at some marshmallow on her skirt. "It's fine actually."

Most people were working on their second helpings when someone began talking about the first Thanksgiving with the Pilgrims and Indians. And that led into a discussion of the early settlers and the first explorers, going all the way back to Columbus.

"I don't see why people give poor old Columbus such a hard time," said a white woman Franklyn recognized but couldn't place until he realized it was Jacquie's piano teacher. "If it hadn't been for Columbus, none of us would be here, right? You know, the Mayflower at Plymouth Rock and all that," she said, leaping ahead about a century and a quarter.

"Honey, I don't think your folks and mine came over on the same boat," Mrs. Cox remarked with a smile. "More turkey, anybody? There's plenty of everything!"

The woman looked a little embarrassed at his mother's gentle reference to the slave ships that brought African captives to America to work on the plantations.

"Sooner or later somebody would have come here," Mrs. Bishop said. "Maybe from Africa, instead of Europe."

"Somebody *did* come from Africa," said Major Cox. "There's a theory that Africans were really the first explorers."

"But if the Africans got here first, they didn't stick around. Something must have happened to them, right?" argued Mr. Burkhardt. "So the Spanish came, and they took what they thought they had a right to from folks who were already here, had been here for maybe thousands of years. And the Europeans killed off a lot of Indians, either on purpose or by giving them diseases that wiped them out. Anyway, it happened, and here we are."

"Yes, indeed, here we are," said Mrs. Cox, "and let's be thankful for what we have. Anybody ready for pie? We've got mince, apple, pumpkin, and pecan."

Franklyn was relieved when his mother changed the subject. Georgia O'Keeffe took the Adams twins to get their pie, and the old black man, who had not said anything during the discussion, hitched his chair closer to Franklyn. "Bet I could tell you some stories," he said, "if you had a mind to listen."

Franklyn glanced up at the old man's deeply weathered face. A couple of fresh gravy spots had joined the old ones on his ancient necktie. "Sure," said Frank.

"You ever hear of George McJunkin?"

Franklyn shook his head.

"Black cowboy," the old man said in a raspy voice. "Born a slave in Texas but ended up working for a ranch in New Mexico, up in Folsom, near Raton. Found some bones there that turned out to be pretty important. That was way back at the turn of the century. Archaeologists came down from Denver, found out George stumbled on something big that proved Indians were around here a lot earlier than anybody believed."

"A black cowboy did that?"

"Yessir, he did. Never got a mite of credit for it, though."

Franklyn thought he might be a cowboy himself someday. His mother had bought him an old pair of spurs at a garage sale, and she promised she'd get him some boots as soon as his feet stopped growing. He was saving money to buy himself a cowboy hat, although Jacquie was the only person who knew that.

"Think you could find me a piece of that pecan pie?" the old man asked. "Then I'll tell you another story, the story of Estebanico."

Franklyn brought them each some pie and settled down again next to the old man's chair. "Who?"

"Estebanico, another black man. You never heard of him, either?"

"No. Who's he?"

The old man shook his head sadly. "Nobody teaching you young folks the things you ought to know." He took up a forkful of pie. "One of the first non-Indians to set foot in what is now New Mexico was a Moorish slave, shipwrecked with his owner, a Spaniard named Dorantes. They say he got killed by the Zuni Indians later on. But I have a theory: What if Estebanico escaped? Who knows? What if his descendants are still around here?"

The old man winked knowingly. "Wouldn't Estebanico have some story to tell? Look it up, young fella. You might find it interesting."

Carefully the old man laid his fork on the empty plate and handed it to Franklyn. "Would you be kind enough to take care of this for me? I must be going. I'm expected someplace else this afternoon. Please express my gratitude to your kind parents."

Jacquelyn brought him his crumpled hat, and Franklyn handed him his cane. The old man made his way slowly to the door. "Good-bye," Franklyn said. "Thank you for coming." They watched him hobble down the street, his cane swinging slowly back and forth in front of him.

After everyone had gone home, taking leftovers with them—Franklyn had helped put together a big package for the Adamses, including the old man's grape jelly—Major Cox sat at the empty dining-room table with a cup of coffee. "Who was that old gentleman, Dorrie?" the major asked his wife, who was putting the turkey platter back in the china cabinet.

"Don't know. Never saw him before. Somebody must have told him he'd get a good meal here. Oh, Lord, I am tired! Franklyn, you were talking to him. Did he tell you his name?"

"Steven," he said. "He didn't tell me his last name."

"Me, either," Jacquelyn said. She had taken off her Georgia O'Keeffe outfit and was fixing herself a turkey sandwich. "Nice old guy."

"He gave me a couple of ideas for my Heritage project. I'm probably going to write about Estebanico, the black explorer."

In the following week, as he worked on his story, Franklyn kept thinking about what the old man had said, that maybe Estebanico hadn't been killed after all. That he had somehow managed to escape, hide out, start a new life somewhere else. Nothing Franklyn read said anything about that, but somehow the old man seemed to *know* something.

And his name was Steven, English for Estevan. For Estebanico. *Just a coincidence,* Franklyn assured himself. Had to be. But from then on, Franklyn kept watch for the Thanksgiving stranger.

ESTEBANICO, BLACK EXPLORER

❖

by Franklyn Cox

O N E of the first people from Europe to
set foot in New Mexico was a black man.
He was an African slave belonging to a Spanish
explorer named Dorantes. He was called Estebanico, or Estevan or Esteban, which are Spanish for
Steven.

Not many people know Estebanico's story. It
begins around 1528, which was thirty-six years after
Columbus landed in America. A lot of things had
happened in those years. Spanish explorers looking
for adventure and riches sailed across the ocean to
explore the land Columbus had found. One of the
first explorers was Hernán Cortés, who conquered
the Aztecs in 1521. He called the land of the Aztecs
New Spain and changed the name of their capital
from Tenochtitlán to Mexico City.

A few years later another group of explorers
sailed for Florida. A Spaniard named Dorantes and
his slave Estebanico were on that expedition. They
did not find riches in Florida, just fierce Indians.
A lot of the explorers died, but the survivors man-

aged to build new boats and tried to sail to New Spain, which we now call Mexico. Their luck was bad, too. They were shipwrecked and many drowned. Dorantes and Estebanico and a few others made it to shore near Galveston, Texas. (Of course there was no city there back then.) They were captured by Indians and made slaves. Pretty soon only fifteen of the whole group that left Spain together were still alive.

By 1534 eleven more Spaniards were dead, but Dorantes, his slave Estebanico, a man named Cabeza de Vaca, and another man managed to escape. Slowly the four men made their way westward. They went from village to village saying they were doctors who could heal the sick and even raise the dead. Along the way they endured terrible hardships and ate all kinds of awful stuff just to stay alive. They walked clear across Texas, New Mexico, and Arizona, and they finally got to Mexico City in the spring of 1536. They were the only survivors of the expedition to Florida.

You can imagine how people reacted to their arrival. The men were treated like kings. Everyone wanted to hear their stories about all they had seen. The Spanish officials expected to hear stories of great riches, like the gold Cortés took from the Aztecs and Pizarro took from the Incas in Peru. Cabeza de Vaca told the officials that the lands they had *crossed were very poor. But no one wanted to believe him. The officials had heard tales of the seven cities of gold somewhere far to the north of Mexico City. They believed those tales and thought that Cabeza de Vaca and his companions must be wrong.*

Three years later the viceroy, a representative appointed by the King of Spain, decided to send a fact-finding party out to look for those cities of gold. But Cabeza de Vaca had already left, and Dorantes, Estebanico's owner, wasn't interested in any more adventure. So the viceroy put a priest, Fray Marcos, in charge of the expedition and picked Estebanico to be his guide.

Estebanico was told to go on ahead and mark a path for Fray Marcos and the rest of the group who would follow. Mainly he was to be on the lookout for the golden cities, which everyone called the Seven Cities of Cíbola (cíbola means "buffalo cow"). Fray Marcos worked out a code: if Estebanico saw a city, he was to send back a messenger with a cross. A small cross meant a small town. Bigger crosses meant bigger cities.

They gave Estebanico a pair of greyhounds and some Indian helpers, and he started off three days ahead of Fray Marcos. He loved to dress up in costumes with feathers and jingle bells and to wear fancy headdresses. He made friends easily with the Indians he met along the way and gave them some of the trinkets he carried with him. Sometimes they invited him to join in their dances and parties. The chief of one friendly tribe gave him a present of a gourd rattle, which was a symbol of authority.

Estebanico didn't find any cities of gold on his journey. All he found were more poor Indian villages. But he must have liked to play jokes because he kept sending crosses back to Fray Marcos, bigger and bigger crosses. The last one was so big it took a burro to carry it.

Then he arrived at the pueblo of the Zunis, on the western border of New Mexico, next to Arizona. But he must have done something to make the Zuni people very angry. Maybe he demanded things from them they didn't want to give him. Or maybe he showed them the gourd rattle, and it turned out to belong to enemies of the Zuni. Nobody knows for sure. The next thing Fray Marcos heard, his guide was dead, shot in the back with arrows.

Fray Marcos hurried back to Mexico City and told the viceroy that he had seen the Seven Cities of Cíbola. This was a lie, but for a while everybody believed it.

There were many more expeditions in New Mexico but no more black explorers. No one ever found cities of gold.

Here is something else I learned about Estebanico. When this state was getting ready to cast a medallion for the Bicentennial celebration of 1976, the organizers planned to celebrate the three cultures of New Mexico—Indian, Anglo, and Hispanic. Then someone suggested it's really four cultures, if you count African-Americans. They wanted to include Estebanico on the medallion. But then the Zunis heard about it and got upset, saying Estebanico was killed because he was evil. They made the organizers take Estebanico off the medallion. No more Estebanico—back to three cultures again.

GEORGIA O'KEEFFE,
AN ARTIST OF NEW MEXICO

❖

by Jacquelyn Cox

G EORGIA O'Keeffe knew by the time she was thirteen that she was going to be an artist. She was born November 15, 1887, in Sun Prairie, Wisconsin, where her parents had a dairy farm and six other children. When she was about eleven, she started taking art lessons from a woman who taught her to copy pictures from a book. But Georgia wanted to work on other things. Flowers were her favorite subjects. And she wanted to work alone.

Then her family sold the farm and moved to Virginia. That's when Georgia began to develop her own style of dressing. She wore plain tailored suits instead of frilly dresses like the other girls. She pulled her hair back and braided it instead of fluffing it out with ribbons, like the others. All her life she dressed in dramatic black clothes and paid no attention to current fashion.

In 1907, when she was twenty years old, Georgia moved to New York City to study at the Art Students League. She began going to art exhibits *arranged by Alfred Stieglitz, a great photographer. Of course she had no idea then that she was going to marry him someday because he was much older than she was and very famous. Besides, he already had a wife.*

Because she had to earn a living, Georgia O'Keeffe went to teach school in Amarillo, Texas, which if you have ever driven across the Panhandle, you know is a very flat place without mountains or trees.

Meanwhile Georgia was sending her artwork to a friend in New York, Anita Pollitzer, telling her not to show the drawings to anyone. But Anita went ahead and showed Georgia's work to Mr. Stieglitz anyway. He loved the drawings and hung some of them in an exhibit. Instead of being pleased when she found out about it, Georgia got angry and told him to take down her drawings, but he talked her into letting them stay up. Actually no one knows if this is a true story or partly a myth.

While Georgia was teaching in Texas, Alfred Stieglitz wrote to her often, and she wrote back. That's how they got to know each other. In 1918 he invited her to move to New York. He began to take lots of photographs of her because she was as beautiful as she was talented. Even though they were falling in love, they argued. He claimed that she was a great woman artist, that her work was different because she was a woman, and she didn't appreciate that. She wanted to be known as an artist regardless of whether she was a man or a woman. Eventually Alfred got a divorce, and Georgia married him on December 11, 1924, even though she was thirty-seven years old and he was sixty and they disagreed about a lot of things.

All this time she painted and painted and painted, pictures of New York City and Lake George, where they went for vacations, as well as her beautiful flowers. There were other women artists then, but Georgia O'Keeffe was the most famous.

In the summer of 1929 Georgia O'Keeffe visited Taos, New Mexico. She learned to drive a car and drove around looking at the rugged mountains and colorful rocks. She loved the brilliant light and the clear air. She painted like mad: mesas, skulls, crosses, adobe churches. From then on she kept going back to New Mexico for months at a time. Georgia had her own life, and Alfred had his.

While she was in New Mexico she met many famous writers and artists, such as the famous photographer Ansel Adams. Often she stayed in an adobe house near Ghost Ranch, a popular dude ranch near the little village of Abiquiú. She had privacy and *wonderful views of the rocks and hills. For many years she divided her time between New Mexico and New York.*

During the 1940s O'Keeffe did many paintings of bones and skulls. She and Alfred didn't spend much time together. They admired each other, but they couldn't stand living together. But she went to see him when he was dying because she truly cared about him. He died July 13, 1946, and she went back to New Mexico, where she bought an old, run-down house in Abiquiú. She fixed it up and planted a garden. But she didn't paint as much as she used to, because she was getting old and her eyesight wasn't good anymore. A young potter, Juan Hamilton, came to help her, and there were rumors that she had married him, even though he was young enough to be her grandson.

Georgia O'Keeffe wanted to live to be a hundred years old, but she didn't make it. She died when she was ninety-eight, on March 7, 1986. However, she did become one of the most famous artists of her time.

RICKY BEGAY

❈

Photography and Other Lessons

RICKY Begay focused the camera on his grandfather, who was hunched over his workbench. *Click* went the shutter; *click, click,* two more shots, just to be sure. Ricky moved the camera to a different angle and took another reading with his light meter. He refocused the lens for a close-up of the old man's hands, veined and gnarled with age. *Tap tap tap* went his grandfather's delicate hammer on the thin silver disk.

The camera was ancient, bought at a pawnshop. It was so old Ricky had to calculate everything: film speed, amount of available light, shutter speed, size of lens opening. He had seen the automatics that did everything for you. All you had to do was point those high-tech jobs and snap the shutter, and the camera figured it all out. Ricky didn't like that kind. His Konica was more interesting and certainly more of a challenge.

Ricky's grandfather, Joe Bennett, wore his long gray hair in the traditional Navajo *chongo,* pulled into a ponytail that was twisted and looped back on itself and bound with a colorful ribbon. As always a couple of turquoise necklaces hung around his neck. The light over his workbench glinted off his eyeglasses. Ricky adjusted the lamp so it wouldn't glare in the pictures. He had used most of a roll of black-and-white film already.

Ricky's idea was to tell the story of a piece of Navajo jewelry from the time his grandfather started working on it until it got sold, all in pictures. "It's a class project," Ricky had explained to him. "We're doing a book about our heritage. Being Indian and all."

His grandfather thought about that. "You going to do the whole book, Ricky?"

"No. Just one chapter."

"You could do a whole book about the Dineh. The People."

"Maybe someday I will."

"Too bad you couldn't take some pictures

of the old *hogan* where I learned," Grandfather said. "Then you'd have the story where it started."

This was where it started for Ricky, too. He had been born on the Navajo reservation up near Shiprock, in the northwest corner of New Mexico. His parents still lived there, and so did two older sisters. Ricky had come down to Albuquerque to live with his grandfather about six months earlier, after his grandmother got sick and died. He was supposed to keep his grandfather company in the little house he moved to after Grandmother died. The new house was so close to the railroad tracks that it sounded as though the trains were roaring right through it. But Grandfather couldn't stay in the old place because, like all Navajo, he was afraid of the dead, and there was the chance that Grandmother's ghost might still haunt their old house. The new house was noisy but safe.

Ricky didn't have the patience to sit at a workbench hour after hour, as Grandfather did, making bolo ties—silver-and-turquoise slides on leather strings. Bolos were popular at Old Town Plaza, where Joe Bennett sold his jewelry. Tourists liked them. Lots of white men wore them instead of a necktie. "Ladies wear them now, too," Grandfather said. "Got to be fashionable, I guess."

Ricky moved in for a close-up of a bolo. This one had a piece of polished turquoise set in an oval of silver stamped with a design around the edge. He watched his grandfather solder a narrow strip of silver to hold the bluish green stone on the silver disk.

"String a bunch of these together, like this," Grandfather said. He opened a drawer in his workbench and pulled out a handsome silver belt. "Concha belt, it's called. I made this one a long time ago. Your grandmother wore it on her velvet skirt. Looked real pretty." He stared at it and laid it aside. Ricky knew it must make his grandfather feel sad.

"They sell for a good bit of money. Kind of tourists I sell to usually don't want to pay that much, so I make the little things, too," Grandfather said.

He reached far back in the drawer. "Now here's something else you might like to make a picture of. Squash-blossom necklace. This crescent-shaped piece here in the middle is a *naja*. They used to hang them on the brow-band of a headstall, the part of a bridle that fits over the horse's head. Then they started putting them on bead necklaces with these little silver squash blossoms in between the beads. My daddy made this necklace. I remember when he used to take it to the pawnshop at the trading post when he needed money, and it would stay there until he wanted to wear it to a dance or a sing or something special, and the trader let him borrow it. Afterward it would go back to the trading post. Everybody did that, I guess. Most people never had the money to get it out of pawn. That's how the best jewelry ended up in white people's collections."

Ricky hung the squash-blossom necklace around his grandfather's neck and took a photograph. Then he took pictures of other pieces of jewelry his grandfather had stashed around the little house, including a woman's squash-blossom necklace that Joe Bennett had made. More delicate than the man's, it had won a ribbon at Indian Market, but so far no one had bought it. It was too expensive.

"In the old days," Grandfather said after a while, "we used to make all kinds of things by sandcasting. I carved a copy of what I wanted to make out of wax and covered it with sand. Then I melted out the wax and poured melted silver into the space the wax left. And there it was—something beautiful.

Buckles, bracelets, things like that. But not anymore. It costs too much, and people don't pay." He picked up his hammer again. *Tap tap tap*.

．　．　．

On the day after Thanksgiving, Grandfather packed up a few of his good pieces and a boxful of the less expensive items, and he and Ricky drove to Old Town Plaza in Joe's rattletrap station wagon. Joe Bennett and several other Indians had permits to sell jewelry under the portal that sheltered the east side of the plaza. They spread blankets on the brick sidewalk and arranged their jewelry for tourists to admire. Joe went there almost every day in summer, which was tourist season, and on winter weekends.

Winter was the slow time. It was cold and not so many tourists came. Most of the Indians stayed home to make jewelry for the big summer season. But Joe Bennett said it was a mistake to give it up entirely. Even in winter he spent time on the plaza on weekends, just in case. Sometimes Ricky went along to help.

Most of the Navajo vendors brought folding chairs to sit on while the tourists filed by slowly, staring down at the jewelry. Sometimes a customer would see something she liked and would stoop down to pick it up and examine it more closely. A lot of the Indians kept little hand mirrors so their customers could see how they looked in the jewelry. Joe arranged his merchandise with care, so that the expensive concha belts and the prize-winning squash-blossom necklace attracted attention, but the cheaper bolos and earrings were in easy reach. He set up little white cards with prices printed on them so customers wouldn't have to ask how much something cost.

Shivering and stamping his feet, Ricky wished he had had this idea for the photographs when the weather was warmer. He and Grandfather had bundled up in heavy jackets and extra socks, for although the weather forecast called for sunshine, the air was definitely chilly. A lot of tourists had come to Albuquerque for the long Thanksgiving weekend, and according to Joe Bennett, the day after Thanksgiving would be a big day.

Joe Bennett had been right. Large numbers of tourists strolled around in a festive mood, soaking up the sunshine. They crisscrossed the plaza, visited the historic San Felipe de Neri Church, and wandered in and out of shops that specialized in T-shirts and souvenirs. A horse and carriage waited on the west side of the plaza to take people for rides through the narrow side streets.

All morning Ricky sat with his grandfather next to their blanket, scanning the steady stream of tourists. Most of them just glanced at the jewelry and kept on going. Some stopped to look more closely, and a few actually bought something.

Some visitors assumed the Indians didn't speak English and talked loudly to make them understand. And Ricky overheard one elderly woman ask, "Do you take American money?"

"You get somebody like that almost every day," Grandfather said with a quiet chuckle when the woman had moved on, clutching her purse. "They don't know they're in the United States. They come to Albuquerque and think they left the country." The man on the blanket next to theirs said, "Maybe they have."

Around noon a man decked out in plaid pants and a bright yellow jacket strolled by. His wife wore a soft suede coat. The man carried an expensive camera slung over his shoulder. Ricky always tried to get a look at the cameras the tourists carried. Grandfather sat impassively, not looking at his customers, letting them decide on their own whether to stop or keep on going, whether to buy or just to look.

"Hey, Chief!" the man said loudly. "You interested in selling some of this stuff?"

Joe Bennett turned slowly to look at him and then turned away again, as though he hadn't heard.

"Hey, listen, Geronimo! You speak a little English, right? So you can talk to your customers once in a while?" The man in the plaid pants leaned closer to Grandfather, his face only a couple of feet from Joe Bennett's proud profile.

Grandfather glanced at the man again. "You buy what you like," he said in his slow, flat voice.

The man's wife picked up the squash-blossom necklace, held it up to her neck, and turned for her husband to see. The man took it from her, examined it, and dropped it carelessly back on the blanket. "Your prices seem way too high. So let's do some bargaining here. I give a little, you give a little, maybe you've got yourself a deal. I'm offering you half what you're asking, okay?"

"No bargaining," Grandfather said. "Prices are fair."

"I go down to Juárez, and they bargain.

You could learn something from the Mexicans." He turned to the other vendors on their blankets, searching for someone to agree with him. "Right?" he kept asking. "Am I right?"

But they were all Navajo; nobody responded or changed expression. They all stared at something off in the distance.

The man finally gave up. He grabbed his wife's arm and steered her away.

Grandfather's face remained as calm as stone. No one said a word.

Not all tourists were so bad, though. In fact, Ricky realized, some tourists were really nice. Three girls about his own age came out of a souvenir shop, their winter jackets unzipped to show off their identical T-shirts with hot-air balloons printed on them. They started to walk past the jewelry, but then they stopped and knelt down to try on some of Grandfather's bolos. *They are sisters,* he decided, *visiting from, ummm, maybe California. They look nice.* One of them glanced up and smiled at him. He wished he had the nerve to talk to the girls and ask if he could take their picture as they tried on some dangling turquoise and silver earrings.

Around noon Ricky and Joe Bennett ate the bologna sandwiches they had brought from home. Ricky had just made up his mind to take some pictures of Grandfather surrounded by his blanketful of jewelry when a family stopped to examine Joe Bennett's work. "We're from Texas," explained the bald-headed man in a fancy photographer's vest with a dozen pockets. "These are our children and grandchildren." He beamed proudly. "We're here to do our Christmas shopping." His wife pulled out a long list, and within a short time they had bought something for everyone on the list.

The Texans had a camera and asked permission to take a picture of Joe Bennett with his jewelry. Then one of the women noticed Ricky sitting by quietly and asked if he would mind taking a picture of their family using their camera.

"My husband will set everything for you," the woman said reassuringly.

Ricky didn't need to have anyone set it for him, but he didn't say anything. *What a beautiful camera,* Ricky thought, taking it carefully from the bald-headed man. He checked the focus while the family—grandparents, parents, and several small children—discussed how to arrange themselves, and then he took several shots while they were still trying to get posed. The little kids looked tired and grumpy. Ricky could see that they didn't want to be doing this, but then something caught their attention and Ricky captured their fleeting expressions of interest.

"Hey, you look right at home with that camera, young man," the bald-headed man said when the session was over. "Are you a photographer?"

Ricky nodded, tongue-tied.

"Maybe you let my grandson take a picture of you with his camera?" Ricky's grandfather asked suddenly. "School project," he added.

"Why, sure thing," the visitors said. "You just tell us what you want us to do."

Ricky got his camera out of its battered leather case. "Pick up something," he began, cleared his throat, and began again. "Would you please pick up something like you're going to buy it? Maybe the squash-blossom necklace?"

The grandmother knelt in front of the blanket and reached for the necklace. Ricky moved in and began clicking off the shots as the woman picked it up, examined it, tried it on, and smiled at her reflection in the hand mirror.

"Hope you're not out of film, son," said

the grandfather, reaching into his hip pocket. "Might as well get a shot of this, too." Obediently, Ricky took a picture of him pulling out his wallet. "Got that?" he asked, winking at Ricky.

Ricky nodded.

"Looks like we're gonna take that necklace, too," the man said, handing a fistful of cash to Joe Bennett.

"You're buying it, Leonard?" the grandmother asked, and Ricky was quick enough to capture the look of surprised pleasure on her face.

"Early Christmas present," the grandfather explained gruffly. He fished a business card out of another compartment of his wallet. "Grateful if you'd send me some prints of those pictures," he said, handing the card to Ricky.

Ricky nodded again, completely speechless, and the customers moved away, waving and smiling. They had just made a lot of money, but his grandfather's expression hadn't changed at all. He merely nodded. The Navajo way.

Meanwhile, the man in the plaid pants and his wife were crossing the plaza. They stopped in the middle, near the gazebo, to discuss something. Ricky decided they were from New York. Someday he was going to visit and see the Empire State Building and the Statue of Liberty. He hoped not everyone from New York was like them.

"I don't like those people," Ricky said. "The man in the plaid pants. He talked to you like you're stupid."

"Like doesn't matter," Grandfather said slowly. After a long pause he went on, "Did I tell you about when I was a boy, not much older than you? I lied about my age and joined the Marines. They made me a code talker and sent me to the Pacific. And the white man who was assigned to work with me didn't like the idea of working with a dumb Indian. Then he found out I wasn't so dumb. Once I saved his life. Once he saved my life. Didn't matter we didn't like each other. That's the way it was." He pointed. "Now, look."

The couple started walking toward them. The woman was smiling, her hand hooked in her husband's arm. Ricky stared at them, braced for more of the white man's rudeness. "We've been talking it over," the man said, "and I'd like to buy that necklace for my wife. That—what do you call it?—squash blossom. Now what's your best price?"

"Sold it," Grandfather said. "At full price," he added.

Ricky saw the woman's smile fade. "Don't you have another one?" she asked. It was the first Ricky had heard her say anything.

"No more." Wordlessly, Joe Bennett leaned forward and straightened the concha belt, just enough to call it to her attention. Then he gazed impassively off into the distance again.

The woman noticed the belt and picked it up. She studied the tooled design and the turquoise insets. Then she clasped it around her waist and turned to show it off to her husband. "Oh, George, look at this! It's exquisite!"

George sighed. He opened his mouth and closed it again. No bargaining, no arguing. He reached for his wallet and paid Joe Bennett for the belt, and the two New Yorkers strolled off, arm in arm.

Grandfather said nothing. Ricky said nothing. It was the Navajo way.

NAVAJO CODE TALKER

✣

As Told to Ricky Begay
by Joe Bennett, His Grandfather

MY *name is Joe Bennett, age sixty-five. I grew up on the Navajo Indian Reservation near Shiprock, New Mexico. I was fifteen when the Japanese bombed Pearl Harbor at the start of World War II. I was herding my family's sheep when a couple of Marines came to the reservation, looking for young men who could speak English and Navajo. They wanted us to join the Marines and be trained to talk in a new code that the Japanese would not be able to crack. They thought the Navajo language was so hard it would fool the enemy. They were right.*

I wanted to be a code talker, so I lied and said I was eighteen. Next thing I knew, I was on a train going to San Diego. Never been away from the reservation, never seen a train, didn't know what was going on. It was like a dream. Didn't have sense enough to be scared. I learned that later.

The Marines were afraid the Japanese might find somebody who understood Navajo, even though it's such a hard language. So they had the men make up a Navajo code. They figured out 211 words, plus a word for each letter of the alphabet. Each word stood for something different from what it means in our language. For instance, our word for "whale" is lotso, *and that was the word they decided to use for "battleship." They kept adding more and more words with mixed-up meanings. We had to memorize what all those words meant. It was a good code. The Japanese never did crack it.*

I was shipped to Guadalcanal. At first the officers didn't know what to do with the code talkers. Then they learned to depend on us. By the end of the war there were about four hundred code talkers. It was dangerous work, and some got killed. One of the big dangers was not from the Japanese. Sometimes the white Marines mistook the Navajos for Japanese spies and wanted to kill us. So a white soldier was sent along as a kind of bodyguard for each code talker in the combat zone.

There were usually two code talkers in each division. One went ashore and the other stayed on the ship. We used our radios to send the officers' messages back and forth, coding and decoding them fast.

I took part in the invasion of Iwo Jima. That was one of the most important battles in the war. The invasion was directed by orders in Navajo code. We sent more than eight hundred messages, but the

Japanese were not able to figure out a single one.

I was sent ashore with a white Marine. We tied ourselves together with a piece of rope so we wouldn't get separated in the dark. We crawled into a foxhole. But then the white Marine got hit, and I had to stay in the foxhole with the dead man and keep sending messages back to the ship. It was hard, because Navajo people are afraid of dead bodies.

When I came home after the war, I and other Navajo soldiers had an "Enemy Way" ceremony to get rid of the bad memories and the ghosts of the dead that haunted us.

For a long time after the war, the code talkers were kept a secret. But we had a fiftieth anniversary celebration at the Pentagon. I went to Washington, D.C., for the celebration. I didn't think I could still remember the code because I'm old and it was all a long time ago, but when somebody sent the message "Give back the ram" in Navajo, I knew what it meant: Acknowledge message.

I am proud of the Navajo code talkers and glad I could serve my country.

REBECCA RIVERA
AND SARA McGINLEY

❖

The Virgin of the
Bosque Road Neighborhood Association

REBECCA Rivera knew she'd make a perfect Virgin Mary, if only the Bosque Road Neighborhood Association would let her.

Ever since she was a little girl, Becky had loved to dress up like the Blessed Virgin, draping her great-aunt Consuelo's blue shawl over her head and shoulders so that just a little bit of her dark hair peeped out from under the veil. Before she even started school, Becky had learned to walk in a dignified manner, eyes lowered modestly, a baby doll representing the Infant Jesus cradled in her arms. In the room she shared with her younger sister, María, she had fixed up a *nacimiento,* a little manger in which to lay her make-believe Baby Jesus. Her parents should have given the name of María to her instead of to her sister!

For years Becky dreamed of being the Virgin Mary in the annual neighborhood Christmas Eve procession of *Las Posadas,* The Inns. Following an old New Mexican custom, a group of people go from house to house, singing traditional songs in Spanish as they accompany Joseph and the Virgin Mary in their search for a place to stay on the night of Jesus' birth. At each "inn" the travelers are turned away, until they reach the last one, where they are welcomed. Playing the role of the Virgin was always a great honor.

Changes in her body last summer signaled that Becky was no longer a child—"You're a young lady now," her mother had said proudly—and Becky felt sure that since she had entered this new stage of her life she would be chosen for the part of the Virgin this year.

Bosque Road was an unusual neighborhood, even for Albuquerque. At the west end where the street stopped at the river, a cluster of high-priced condos was hidden behind a fake adobe security fence with a locked iron gate. At the east end near Rio Grande Boulevard stood a mobile home park called Piñon Acres. In the half dozen blocks between were all kinds of houses, some ordinary and some pretty unusual, like the one with a real live tree growing up through the roof where Becky's best friend, Sara McGinley, lived. The McGinleys' house was surrounded by a couple of acres of land stretching all the way to the ditch bank.

Becky's parents and grandparents lived at the west end, next door to each other in two plain square houses with apricot trees in the small front yard. Her grandfather had painted both houses a vivid shade of pink. Everyone in the family thought it looked very nice. But one day a couple of people from the condos in the walled-in compound across the street came to visit and asked if they would consider repainting the houses "to a more natural adobe color" if the condo residents chipped in and bought the paint. The houses had remained pink.

In the narrow strip of ground between the pink houses an old bathtub stood on end, faucet end down. Inside the tub Becky's Tía Consuelo had placed a statue of the Virgin of Guadalupe, dressed in a blue robe and surrounded by plastic roses. Real vines twined around the bottom of the shrine, and a pair of votive candles in tall glass jars sat in front. When they were little girls Sara and Becky used to bring gifts—a pretty stone, a button, an old earring—for the statue. When they were older, Becky learned the legend of the Virgin of Guadalupe from her uncle Rolando, who was a priest in El Paso, and she told Sara the miraculous story.

"Long ago on a hillside in Mexico the Virgin Mary appeared to an Indian peasant named Juan Diego. Every time he saw her, she spoke to him. But when Juan told his priest that he had seen the Virgin and she had talked to him, the priest didn't believe him. The next time Juan saw the Virgin he asked her to give him a sign to take to the priest. The Virgin said, 'Hold up your apron'—this kind of gunnysack around his waist that peasants wore—and she filled it with roses, even though it was winter and no roses were blooming. Juan ran back to the church and spilled out his apronful of roses in front of the priest. And there on the apron was a beautiful image of the Virgin. So the priest had to believe him, and the hill where the peasant saw the Virgin was named Guadalupe, after her shrine in Spain."

"What a beautiful story," Sara said with a sigh. "Catholics have all the best stories."

Sara didn't seem to know anything about the Virgin Mary and Jesus and all the saints, but Becky enjoyed teaching her. She would never forget the day Sara told her, "We're not Catholic. We don't go to church at all."

Sara's admission that on Sunday morning she and her family went not to church but to the Frontier Restaurant for breakfast had stunned Becky. Everybody in her family went together to mass every Sunday and on all the major feast days. Tía Consuelo was even more devout—she attended mass every day. Sometimes at family gatherings Father Rolando suggested that Becky might want to think about becoming a nun when she was older. Being a nun didn't interest Becky. She just wanted to continue to make special devotions to the Blessed Mother. And to play the part of the Virgin in *Las Posadas*.

When Becky confided to Sara her deepest wish, Sara was both sympathetic and practical. "Why don't you just tell them you want to do it?" Sara asked.

"It's not that simple," Becky explained. "What if Denise García wants to do it again?"

Denise, another girl in the neighborhood who was a tenth grader at Valley High, had been the Virgin for the last three years. Denise inherited the role from her sister Danielle, who was the Virgin for three years before that. The main thing Denise had going for her was that the García sisters' grandfather had started the custom of *Las Posadas* on Bosque Road years ago. Everyone assumed the part belonged to his granddaughters. But Denise, like Danielle, had already had her big *quinceañera* party for her fifteenth birthday with a special mass and dinner dance afterward. In Becky's opinion Denise was already too old. Becky believed it was her turn to be the Virgin, now that she was, in her mother's words, "a young lady."

Becky's mother tried to reason with her. "You'll get your turn next year, or the year after. You're only twelve, Rebecca. Be patient! You have plenty of time for this. Let the other girl have her chance, *mi hijita*."

"She's had her chance," Becky muttered.

Even Sara counseled patience. "Don't worry, we'll figure something out," Sara had said soothingly in August and again in September and was still saying in October. "Denise as the Virgin is practically history."

But Becky was in no mood for patience, or for waiting for another year. She knew that Denise García with her bright makeup and her hair that stood up stiff as a rake had never been even half as serious as she, Becky, was about the role. She would bet anything that Denise hadn't been playing dress-up Virgin since she was a child. Day after day Becky tried to think of a way to get Denise out of the picture and herself in. Then Sara called one day with unbelievably good news.

"We just got two burros," Sara said. "Want to come and see them?"

Becky rushed to Sara's house, and the girls climbed on a fence rail and watched the donkeys quietly munching hay. "The big one is Barney and the smaller one is Wilma," Sara explained. "We got them to take up into the mountains on backpacking trips. Won't that be fun?"

The McGinleys were outdoorsy people, and they often invited Becky along on their excursions. They owned a kayak for running the river near Taos when it was deep and fast with spring snowmelt. They skied at Sandía Crest on the east side of the mountains, and one day when there had been an especially heavy snowfall, Becky had looked out her

front window to see the red-headed Mc-
Ginleys whizzing down Bosque Road on
cross-country skis. Now they had burros for
backpacking.

Becky wasn't interested in taking a burro
into the wilderness. But she knew immediately
that one of these animals was her ticket to the
main role in *Las Posadas.* "Up north where
my Tía Consuelo comes from," Becky told
her friend, "the Virgin Mary always rode a
burro in *Las Posadas.* If I could borrow yours,
they'll have to let me be the Virgin."

"I'll ask my parents," Sara said. "But I'm
sure they'll approve. My dad's definitely into
this traditional stuff. I told you we'd think of
something to get rid of Denise, didn't I?"

"You were right," Becky said, trying not
to gloat. She felt she was already as good as
chosen.

There was only one problem. What Becky
didn't want to admit to Sara, and hardly even
to herself, was that she was scared of the burro.
She'd been scared ever since she fell off a horse
when she was small, and even this gentle-eyed
little donkey frightened her. *Well,* she told
herself, *I'll have to get over it before Christmas
Eve, that's all.*

Not only did Sara's parents approve but

Mr. McGinley even offered to help them set up a real manger for the Christ Child in the shed he had built for the donkeys.

When Sara passed along the invitation, Becky turned it down. "The *nacimiento* should be in my grandpa's yard," she announced, although she hadn't yet told her grandparents this. "After all, we have a shrine."

But Sara could be stubborn, too. "I think it ought to be at my place because *A,* it's our burro, and *B,* I'm going to be what's-his-name, Jesus' father—Joseph."

Becky stared at her, aghast. *"You?* You're going to be Saint Joseph? But you can't!"

"Why not?"

Becky could think of several reasons why not. Not only was Sara not Catholic but she didn't know even the most basic things. For instance, Sara didn't seem to understand that Joseph wasn't Jesus' actual father. *God* was Jesus' father! But Becky fell back on the most obvious reason: "A girl can't play the role of Saint Joseph. It's a boy's part," she said.

Sara laughed. "So what? I'll wear one of those towel things over my head, and who's going to know the difference?"

What Becky didn't say was that she thought Joey Baca, who lived in Piñon Acres, should be the one to play Saint Joseph. She had been dreaming about how nice it would be to have Joey leading the burro. He even had the right name! But she didn't think she ought to say too much about this because it wouldn't be quite proper for the girl who was playing the Blessed Virgin to be thinking so much about boys.

But after mulling over Sara's suggestion, she decided maybe it wasn't such a bad idea after all, having her best friend lead the burro. And if this is what it took to get the part, it was a sacrifice she'd gladly make. The idea of sacrificing something appealed to her. It made her more saintly.

When Becky told her mother about the burro, Mrs. Rivera agreed to talk to Mr. García and tell him how much Becky wanted the part. "But I thought you were scared of burros," her mother said.

"Not anymore," Becky said firmly, trying to convince herself, too.

Shortly before Christmas, notices appeared in the mailboxes up and down Bosque Road, announcing a get-together to practice the songs for *Las Posadas* at the Garcías' house. And finally Mr. García himself phoned to ask

Becky if she'd be willing to take the part of the Blessed Virgin in the procession.

Most of the time Becky was ecstatic. This was the moment she had been waiting for. She announced her good news to the Heritage Project class and invited everybody to come. She went to sleep smiling at night, remembering, of course, to say her prayers and to thank the Virgin for granting her biggest wish. She added a new prayer: "Please help me not to be scared of Wilma."

Every afternoon after school Becky went home with Sara, and every afternoon she tried to get up her nerve at least to pet the burro. "You better get used to riding her around the corral," Sara said.

"I will, don't worry," Becky assured her, backing away.

Then, suddenly, it was the day before Christmas. The day Becky had been yearning for had arrived, and she was filled with dread.

Starting early in the morning, the neighbors started to set up the luminarias, papersack lanterns with candles glowing inside. This was a custom that went back before anyone started doing *Las Posadas,* and now it was an official Bosque Road Neighborhood

Association project. Mr. McGinley was in charge. Each year he collected money for the luminaria fund, which he then used to buy a truckload of sand, hundreds of candles at wholesale prices, and hundreds of brown paper sacks. He gave the materials to anybody in the neighborhood who wanted to help.

This year Sara enlisted the kids in the Heritage Project to come and help out, and Mr. McGinley agreed to supply hot cider and *bizcochitos,* little cookies, for the workers. Joey Baca was the first to arrive. Teresa Chávez and Tony Martínez and Tomás Jaramillo and Rosa Gonzales—who all lived nearby—also came early. April Ellis took the bus down from the far North Valley. Even Jeremy Steinberg, who Becky knew was Jewish and probably didn't get involved in Christmas observances, showed up. "I love *bizcochitos,*" Jeremy explained, grinning.

The weather had turned cold and blustery. Dark, fleecy clouds flocked together to hide the sun. All day the workers cuffed paper lunch sacks, dumped sand in each one, and planted a candle in the sand. Their noses turned red and drippy, and their hands were numb with cold.

Everybody on the street would have at

least a few luminarias for Christmas Eve. The McGinleys alone had put almost three hundred paper lanterns along the parapets of their roof and on both sides of the sidewalk leading to their front door. Most important, all the "inns" along the route of *Las Posadas* would have hundreds of lanterns lighting the path for the procession to follow. Even the people in the condos got into the spirit and invited everyone to come to their compound for hot chocolate when the procession ended.

One person who hadn't spent the whole day setting up luminarias was Becky Rivera. She felt that in view of the importance of the role she was to play later that evening, she ought to stay inside and rest. Besides, she was a nervous wreck. Every time Sara had wanted her to get on the burro, she had refused. "I'll do it when the time comes," she had said. Now the time had nearly come. Her stomach ached and her head throbbed.

At four o'clock people began scrambling to get the candles lit in their luminarias. By five o'clock, as darkness fell, the entire length of Bosque Road had been transformed by hundreds or maybe thousands of glowing lights. Becky forced herself to go out and look. *"¡Feliz Navidad!"* neighbors called out to each other. "Merry Christmas!" Everyone seemed touched by the magic—everyone but Becky.

When it was time to get ready, Becky's mother insisted that she put on her brother's long underwear plus heavy socks and an extra sweater under the flowing white robe. She took a pair of woolen gloves and stuffed them up inside the long, full sleeves, just in case Becky's hands got too cold. When Becky protested, her mother reasoned, "If Jesus had been born in New Mexico, you can be sure his mama would have dressed up good and warm." Then she added, "And she would have eaten a decent supper first, too."

Becky shook her head. "I'm fasting." It sounded like a good excuse; the truth was she knew she'd throw up if she ate even one mouthful.

They had decided to start the procession from the McGinleys', since that was Wilma's home, and to wind up at the Garcías', as they always had. Becky was disappointed about that, but she decided it was another sacrifice.

She hardly recognized Sara, buried in baggy black pants and her father's big denim work shirt. Her curly red hair was completely hidden beneath a large bath towel draped over her head and secured low over her eyebrows with a headband. A fake red beard bristled from her chin and flowed down over her chest.

Everybody stood around stamping their feet, trying to keep warm. The clouds had drifted away, revealing a field of brilliant stars, and the air was clear as crystal. *It would have been nice if it had snowed,* Becky thought as Sara adjusted Wilma's halter. Sometimes you got snow for Christmas in Albuquerque, and sometimes you didn't.

It was time to begin. Becky's breath came too fast. She felt light-headed, dizzy with fear, when Mr. McGinley came and boosted her up on the burro's back. "Here you go," he said. Becky grabbed a fistful of Wilma's short mane. "Okay," Mr. McGinley said, "let's move 'em out."

Sara grinned up at her from behind the frizzy red beard. "Ready, Virgin?"

"Uh-huh," Becky croaked miserably.

Sara clucked at Wilma, who took a couple of balking steps. Immediately the Virgin flung her arms around the burro's neck, her eyes squeezed shut, and buried her face in Wilma's mane. Abruptly the burro stopped in its tracks. Becky heard Saint Joseph cluck again.

"Come *on,* Wilma!" Saint Joseph urged, but the animal didn't move. Sara yanked on the reins. Nothing. The singers, who had started the first hymn, faltered, wondering why the procession wasn't going anywhere.

"What's the matter with the burro?" somebody asked.

"I don't know," Saint Joseph replied. "She just won't budge." More clucking, more cajoling, but Wilma stood her ground.

Cautiously Becky loosened her grip on Wilma's neck and dared to open her eyes. For a moment she forgot how scared she was and looked around. Candles flickered everywhere like stars. It was beautiful!

Mr. McGinley appeared. "Trouble?" he asked.

"She won't go," Saint Joseph grumbled and handed the reins to her father.

The singers started the hymn again, a little less enthusiastically this time. "Stop!" Mr. McGinley ordered, and the music trailed off to silence. "Maybe that's what's bothering her. She's not used to singing."

With much effort, Mr. McGinley finally succeeded in dragging the reluctant burro a couple of steps. Becky gasped and clutched frantically at Wilma's mane. Finally Mr. McGinley gave up. "It's no use," he said. "I think it's the lights. This beast just isn't broke to walk through all this candlelight."

"Might as well get down, Virgin," Sara said, and helped Becky to slide off the burro's back.

Becky felt enormous relief and equal frustration as Mr. McGinley led Wilma back to the corral. "What are we going to *do?*" she wailed.

Sara threw her arm around Becky's shoulders. "Walk, I guess," she answered. "Let's go."

At that moment Joey Baca stepped forward, wheeling a shiny black-and-silver bicycle. "You could ride this," he said.

"The Virgin riding a *bike?*" Becky cried. Nothing was working out the way she had dreamed.

"Why not?" Joey asked. "It's brand-new. I just got it for Christmas. I've hardly even ridden it." He smiled at her. One of his front teeth was chipped.

His smile is very nice, Becky thought. *Even with the chipped tooth.* Especially *with the chipped tooth.*

"Hey, why not?" somebody called from the group of singers. "Come on, Becky, do it!"

"Here," said Sara, stripping off the red beard and bath towel and handing them to Joey. "Whoever supplies the transportation gets to be Joseph. I'll walk along with you and be the angel. There's got to be an angel, right?"

"Do it! Do it!" chanted the singers.

Saint Joseph held his bike steady while the Virgin climbed on and arranged her robe and her veil. Joey pushed the bike forward, and Becky grabbed the handlebars for balance. The singers started the hymn again, and the procession moved toward the first house, where a group waited with Lucifer, the devil, played by Mr. García, to turn them away.

Las Posadas had begun. The Virgin let go of the handlebars and rode forth, hands folded serenely in her lap, Saint Joseph at her side guiding the bike, the Angel Sara following protectively after them.

HOW TO MAKE A LUMINARIA

❧

by Rebecca Rivera

I N the old days people built bonfires to light the way for the Holy Family as they looked for shelter on Christmas Eve. Those fires were called luminarias. When traders brought paper sacks to towns along the Santa Fe Trail, people began setting out the sacks with lighted candles inside instead of building bonfires. Some people call the sack-lights farolitos, *which means "little lanterns," but most just call them luminarias. It's a very pretty sight to see a house lit up with hundreds of luminarias.*

To make a luminaria, you need a brown paper lunch bag, a short, stubby candle, such as a votive candle, and some sand (although some people use kitty litter or plain dirt—anything that won't burn.)

1. Open the bag and turn down a cuff around the top about two inches wide.
2. Put a couple of inches of the sand or dirt in

the bottom of the bag. This keeps it from falling over and also prevents fires.

3. Set a candle in the sand.

4. Arrange the luminarias about a foot apart all along the sidewalk leading up to your house or wherever else you think they will look good. The more you have, the more spectacular the sight.

5. About sunset on Christmas Eve, start lighting the candles with a long wooden match. If you have a lot of luminarias, you'll need people to help you. The candles will burn inside the bags for hours. Finally they will go out by themselves. The paper bag keeps the candle from blowing out, but if it rains or snows or gets very windy, it will probably go out anyway. Hope for a nice clear, cold Christmas Eve.

• • •

¡Feliz Navidad!

RECIPE FOR BIZCOCHITOS

⊠

by Sara McGinley

BIZCOCHITOS *are the state cookie of New Mexico. Anise, which tastes like licorice, is what makes them special.*

You need two mixing bowls, measuring cups and spoons, mixing spoons, rolling pin, knife or cookie cutter, small dish, baking sheets, spatula, rack for cooling, and these ingredients:

    ½ cup soft shortening
    ½ cup butter or margarine
    ½ cup sugar
    1 egg
    3 cups flour
    1½ teaspoons baking powder
    ½ teaspoon salt
    1 teaspoon anise seed
    3 tablespoons milk

    TOPPING:

    ¼ cup sugar
    2 teaspoons cinnamon

Sara McGinley

- Preheat the oven to 350 degrees.
- In a large bowl mix the shortening and butter or margarine together with your hands to make the mixture soft and creamy.
- Mix in the sugar with your hands.
- Add the egg and beat the mixture with a spoon until it is fluffy.
- Mix the flour, baking powder, and salt together in another bowl. Add the flour mixture to the shortening and sugar mixture, add the anise seeds, and mix it all together with your hands. The mixture will be crumbly.
- Stir the milk into the mixture. Form the dough into four balls.
- Dust a little flour on a countertop and on a rolling pin. Roll out a ball of dough to about ¼ inch thick. Use a cookie cutter dipped in flour to make fancy shapes or cut the dough into small squares or diamonds with a knife. Put them on a baking sheet.
- For the topping, mix the cinnamon and sugar in a small dish and sprinkle a little on top of each cookie.
- Bake the cookies for 15 to 20 minutes, until they are light brown. Lift them off the baking sheet with the spatula and put them on a rack to cool. Store them in an airtight box, although they are so delicious you won't have to store them very long.

ROSA GONZALES

Another Ghost Story

ROSA Gonzales set her tray down at her usual table in the cafetorium. Every day she ate with the same group of girls who had been her friends all through elementary school and had come to Rio Grande School together last year: Teresa Chávez and Sandra Vargas, who were in the Heritage Project, and Cathy Mondragón and Michelle Cruz, who were taking an advanced math class. They called themselves the Lunch Munch Bunch. Today Teresa was trying to recruit volunteers to come to her house after school and paint her bedroom.

"What color did you get?" Rosa asked.

"Red. The color of dried blood. It'll be very dramatic."

"Your mother said you could?"

"I'm going to surprise her," Teresa said. "That's why I need help, so I can get it done this afternoon before she gets home from work."

But nobody was volunteering. "Can't," Cathy said. "I have a detention. I was late for school this morning, and I have to stay after."

"How come you were late?" Rosa asked. "You live practically next door to the school."

Cathy leaned across the table and said quietly, "*La Llorona* was chasing me last night, and I was so scared I didn't fall asleep until almost four o'clock this morning."

Rosa started to laugh at this ridiculous excuse—*La Llorona,* The Wailing Woman. She was about to ask what Mrs. Salazar had to say to Cathy about blaming a ghost for making her late. But the other girls all stopped eating and gazed intently at Cathy, wanting to hear more.

"Really? You really *saw* her? What did she look like?"

In a hushed voice Cathy described how a woman dressed all in black with long fingernails like polished tin had followed her home from her friend's house. "I was late, I was supposed to be home by nine, but we were watching a video and I forgot what time it was, so I was hurrying. And then I got this feeling, like somebody was following me. I walked faster, *she* walked faster! And then she started wailing real loud, *"Aaayiiieee,"* like that. It gives me goosebumps to think about it! And I ran the rest of the way home and slammed the door and locked it and ran to my room and pushed a chair against the door, but I could still hear her. Then I was too scared to shut my eyes because I kept thinking she was going to get into my room somehow."

The girls seemed to be enthralled as Cathy told her story—all but Rosa, who smiled tolerantly. She had heard of *La Llorona,* of course. She was the most famous ghost in New Mexico. But Rosa had never believed those stories.

Then Teresa Chávez told about the time she and her brother Roberto had been playing by the *acequia,* and they thought they heard *La Llorona.*

" '¡Mis hijos! ¿Dónde están mis hijos?' we heard her say," Teresa insisted. " 'My children! Where are my children?' "

Just the kind of thing you'd expect Teresa to come up with, Rosa thought to herself.

"Did you *see* her?" Sandra demanded. "Actually *see* her? Did she have that horse face, like they say she does?"

"I'm not sure, to tell the truth. I was too scared to look!"

After lunch Rosa got out her special red notebook in which she wrote down her story ideas. Rosa's father anchored the six and ten o'clock local TV news, her mother was the arts editor of the newspaper, and Rosa had decided to follow in her parents' career footsteps. Her notebook usually had at least three or four ideas that she was currently working on, such as her notes for the article on tortillas for the Heritage Project book.

She started a new page titled *"La Llorona."* She jotted down Cathy's story about the Wailing Woman, adding a second paragraph for Teresa's tale. This, Rosa decided, was potentially more interesting than the article about tortillas. She would interview as many people as possible and learn all she could about *La Llorona.*

"Sure, I know the story of *La Llorona,*" her mother said at dinner Sunday night. "It's an old legend, about a ghostly woman who wanders along the rivers and *acequias,* crying for her missing children."

"But who was she? What happened to her children?" Rosa asked. "Did she ever find them?"

"She drowned them, *mi hijita!*"

Rosa's father, who grew up in the valley in south Texas where the Rio Grande forms the boundary between the United States and Mexico, had a more detailed explanation. "The legend goes all the way back to Hernán Cortés, the conqueror of the Aztecs of Mexico in the sixteenth century. Cortés was in love with a beautiful young Aztec maiden who acted as his interpreter. She's called *La Malinche,* which means 'The Tongue.'" Rosa scribbled madly in her notebook. "The story goes that Cortés was the father of her child, but eventually he returned to his wife in Spain. And *La Malinche,* they say, went mad with grief and jealousy and killed her child. The Mexicans regard her as a traitor because she betrayed them to the Spanish conqueror."

"I don't get it," Rosa said. "How did *La Malinche* become *La Llorona?*"

"Because there are lots of ways to tell the story," her father said.

"It's what happens when a young girl gets

involved with a man who doesn't really respect her," her mother interrupted. "The way I heard it from my mother, a peasant girl named María fell in love with a wealthy young man, and they lived together and had children together, but without getting married. Then one day the young man's parents started pressuring him to marry a suitable lady so they would have grandchildren. They didn't know anything about María and the children he already had. Eventually he gave in and told María he must marry someone else, but he promised her he'd come and visit her and the children whenever he could."

"What a wimp!" Rosa said, outraged. "She should have told him to go jump."

"Well, maybe, but remember this is an old story. Girls in the old days weren't likely to do that. And what she did was much, much worse. She went to his wedding to the rich girl and stood in the back of the church with her shawl wrapped around her"——Rosa's mother grabbed a black sweater and threw it over her head to dramatize her story——"and watched while her lover married someone else. María was so jealous and upset she went crazy, and after the ceremony, she ran all the way back to her little house where her children were sleeping, and she killed them."

"How?" Rosa asked breathlessly.

"She threw them into the river."

"The Rio Grande?"

"In this version, yes. And then she jumped in after them and drowned herself."

"Is that the end? Did her no-good boyfriend find out what happened and kill himself, too?"

"I don't think so. But here's what they say happened: After María died, her soul went up to Heaven, and *El Señor*, The Lord, asked her where her children were. She replied that she didn't know. So God wouldn't let her into Heaven."

" 'Go and bring them hither,' " Rosa's father added, imitating God's booming bass voice. " 'You cannot rest until they have been found.' And ever since then, María's ghost has been wandering along the river and the *acequias,* weeping and wailing and calling for her lost children."

"That's not all," Rosa's mom continued. "They say she takes revenge against any man she runs into during her wanderings because a man was the cause of all her troubles."

Rosa wrote it all down in her notebook. The next day she decided to interview Mrs. Salazar. "Do you know the story of *La Llorona*?" she asked the school principal.

"You bet I do. I practically grew up on that story! My people were from near Santa Fe, and the story my mother used to tell me was about a young girl named María who was interested only in pretty clothes. This María was not at all concerned with getting an education but only in finding a handsome husband. And then she met Gregorio, a cowboy from the *llano,* the plains east of the mountains. Not only was he handsome but also very brave: he would ride only half-broken horses. The two good-looking people fell in love and married and had beautiful children, but it wasn't long before Gregorio got restless and began to flirt with other women. And María got so jealous that she turned her anger against those children who looked so much like their father and threw them into the river."

Rosa wrote rapidly, trying to keep up with the principal's story.

"And then, the story goes, she immediately felt sorry for what she had done and tried to get them back, running along the riverbank as the current swept them out of her reach.

But she tripped and fell, hitting her head, and she died from the blow. When her family found her body, the priest refused to bury her in the *camposanto,* the cemetery, and insisted that she be buried by the river. After that it was said she could be seen night after night walking along the riverbank, dressed like a corpse in a long white sheet. And people claimed they heard her crying in a voice like the wind, *'Aaayiiieee . . . mis hijos . . . ¿Dónde están mis hijos?' "*

"My mother used to tell me that story for a couple of reasons," Mrs. Salazar went on. "When I was a little girl, it was to warn me not to stay out after dark or *La Llorona* might snatch me up and carry me away, thinking I was one of her lost children. When I got older, Mama told me the story so I wouldn't make a mistake and forget about my education and marry a man like Gregorio." Mrs. Salazar laughed. "The funny thing is, my husband's name is Gregorio, but he isn't at all like the one in the story!"

The notes in Rosa's book grew longer. She even thought of interviewing the Anglo kids in her class. When she asked Jeremy Steinberg if he had ever heard of *La Llorona,* he looked puzzled. "Yorona? It sounds like it might be a Jewish name, but I'm not sure. I'll ask my mom."

And when Rosa spoke to April Ellis, who lived near the river, April thought it was the machine her father rented to clean out the irrigation ditches in the spring. "Something about a Ditch Witch, I think," she said.

On the other hand, all the Hispanic kids knew the story. Some, like Cathy, had actually been scared by her. Sandra Vargas said her mother had told her *La Llorona* turns people into frogs. "She might even *be* a frog," Sandra said.

Rosa wrote it all down.

When she asked Joey Baca, he told her to meet him after school. "I'll only tell you my story if you promise not to tell," he said as they walked slowly away from the school, toward Rosa's street.

Rosa promised.

"You're not going to believe this," he continued in a low voice, "but she almost got me."

"La Llorona?"

"Yes! See, I never believed in stuff like this. I always figured my mama and my *abuela* made it up to scare me because I used to sneak out at night. One night a couple of years ago my parents went out and my older sister was supposed to be watching out for me, but she wanted to talk to her boyfriend, and she said I could do whatever I wanted to, long as I came home before dark. I got to playing down by the ditch, waiting to see if that old muskrat would stick his nose up. I was having a great time, but then I started getting hungry, and I realized it was late and I better get home before I got in trouble. But it turned out I already was in trouble!"

Rosa leaned encouragingly toward Joey. "And then what happened?"

"I looked up, and there was this white *thing,* coming right toward me. And I turned around and tried to run, but it was like my feet were stuck to the ground, like in a bad dream, you know?"

Rosa nodded.

"And this woman, she had a horrible face, actually no face at all, just a blank, and long, long fingernails that looked like they were dripping blood, and she said, *'Mi hijo,'* kind of moaning. Then she grabbed hold of my shoulder, and it felt like icicles, her fingers were so cold. And she wouldn't let go! I tried to scream or yell for help, and then just like that she let go of me and vanished into thin air. And I ran all the way home."

"You're sure this happened, Joey? You weren't just dreaming or something?"

"No, and I'll tell you why. When I got home I found five round marks like blood-stains on the shoulder of my shirt where she grabbed hold of me. I tried to wash them out, but they wouldn't go away. So I took the shirt out to the backyard and buried it under a bush."

Rosa jumped on the idea. "You think it's still there, under the bush? Could we go and dig it up?"

"That was in another house. We moved away. Somebody else lives there now."

Rosa was disappointed. It would have been wonderful to have proof!

Maybe, she decided, *I'll get the proof I need myself.* The more she thought about it, the more the idea fascinated her. All these other people had seen *La Llorona,* and Rosa hadn't. Why just take other people's word for it? Why not be a real investigative reporter and go looking for *La Llorona* herself?

Rosa's chance came a few nights later when her parents told her they were assigned to cover an important opening at the Albuquerque Museum that weekend. Her brothers were going to sleep over at a friend's house.

"Shall I ask Mrs. Reyes to come and stay with you?" her mother asked.

"Of course not," Rosa said. "I'm perfectly capable of taking care of myself."

"It's not a case of being capable. I just don't want you to feel lonely. Maybe one of your girlfriends could come over? We'd pick her up and take her home again."

"I'll ask," Rosa said, although she didn't want to. She wasn't used to staying home completely alone, but it seemed like an exciting idea. And this could be her night to find *La Llorona*. When the night arrived, she still hadn't bothered to ask anyone to come over.

"You're sure you don't mind staying by yourself?" Mom asked, putting the last touches on her makeup. "We won't be too late."

"We'll call you every once in a while," Dad promised.

"Of course I don't mind." Rosa was annoyed when her parents treated her as though she were a mere child. "I prefer it."

As soon as her parents had driven off, Rosa walked slowly through the empty house, enjoying the luxury of having the place to herself. The only sound was the hum of the refrigerator, and that reminded her that she had also insisted she would fix her own dinner. But first she assembled the equipment she would need later when she set out to find *La Llorona:* camera, to take her picture; tape recorder, to record her wails; red notebook and pencil for jotting impressions; thermos of orange juice, in case she got thirsty waiting for the ghost to show up. Rosa planned to leave as soon as she had eaten.

Imagining that she already had a job as a TV newscaster and lived in her own apartment, she set the table in the dining room with the good china and even a linen napkin. It seemed to have gotten dark early, and Rosa turned on the brass chandelier. She looked out the window and saw that a storm was moving in. Thunder rumbled in the distance. Going out in search of the Wailing Woman no longer seemed like such a good idea. Maybe she'd call Teresa or Michelle and see if one of them wanted to come over.

Then the two bassets, Nippy and Toasty, began howling and whining in the fenced-in backyard. Toasty was a real chicken about staying outside when there was the least sign of rain, but Nippy didn't seem to mind anything. Rosa opened the door, and Toasty dashed past her, diving for the dog bed in the corner of the family room. But where was Nippy?

Rosa called him. No response. She stepped outside, the wind whipping her hair into her face. Then she noticed that the gate was swinging open. Nippy had a bad reputation for taking off whenever he had a chance and had already been hit once by a car. He didn't seem to have learned anything from the experience.

The temperature had dropped, but Rosa didn't bother to go back for a jacket. She jogged down the street, calling the dog. "Here, Nippy!" Finally she spotted him, nose to the ground, headed for the wooded area near the river. "Nippy, come here," she coaxed sweetly, but the dog dodged away. It was going to be a game, she could see that. "Come on, you bad dog!" she ordered. Ignoring her, the dog trotted into the dense trees and was gone.

Stupid dog! It was starting to rain now, and Rosa was shivering. If it weren't for Nippy, she'd be home right now, enjoying the pasta she had planned to fix.

Rosa followed one of the narrow trails into the woods, calling and calling, but the dog had vanished. She hesitated. It was so dark Rosa could hardly see a thing, and she knew she had no business being in the woods alone. Her parents would have a fit if they knew. But she didn't want to leave without Nippy.

Stories of *La Llorona* flashed into her mind. *Well,* she thought bravely, *here I am, Rosa Gonzales, wailing for my dog.*

Then she saw something out of the corner of her eye, something moving . . . something dark, as if it was dressed in black. And she could hear this . . . this awful noise. It sounded like somebody sobbing . . . wailing. She had to get out of there!

Rosa turned and started to run, blindly brushing against a bush. The branches slapped her face. She let out a shriek and bolted for home, forgetting about the dog, forgetting everything but escaping from whatever it was back there in the woods. She was crying. She couldn't help it—she had never been so scared!

When she reached her house, breathless and sobbing, there on the doorstep sat Nippy, tongue lolling, tail thumping, welcoming her home. Stupid animal! She hugged him, and he followed her inside.

Rosa deadbolted the door and hurried from room to room, switching on all the lights. She turned on the television, just to hear the sound of a human voice. When the phone rang, she raced to pick it up on the second ring.

"How are you doing, Rosita?" her dad asked.

His voice sounded so good! "Oh, fine," she said, trying to seem offhand and casual.

"Not scared there in the big house?"

"Of course not!" He must think she was a baby or something.

"We'll see you soon, then!"

Rosa decided to eat her pasta in front of the TV, the dogs curled up next to her. Nippy did seem kind of nervous, she thought, as though he had seen something, or heard something, that scared him, too.

After dinner she got her red notebook out of the backpack where it was tucked next to her camera and tape recorder. But she decided not to work on the story of *La Llorona* tonight. She'd write about tortillas instead.

TORTILLA HISTORY

❖

By Rosa Gonzales

To tell the story of the tortilla, which is like a thin pancake made of ground corn (pronounced tor-TEE-yah, not tor-TILL-uh), I shall begin with the story of corn.

Corn is a New World food. The earliest Indians in what later became New Mexico were nomads who roamed around killing animals for food. But when they learned to grow corn and dry it so they would have food to last them through the winter, their way of life was changed. They could stay in one place and farm.

Later, when the Spanish conquistadores came to this land, corn was one of the first foods they found. The Indians taught the Spaniards how to grow corn. The Spaniards called this new food maíz, which is "maize" in English. There are many different kinds of corn. It even comes in colors, such as blue.

There were two ways to prepare corn for making tortillas. The first way, women cooked dry white corn in lime water until the hulls were loosened. This was called nixtamal. *After they washed it to get rid of the lime, they spread the corn on a slab of volcanic rock, called a* metate, *and rolled a smaller rock shaped like a rolling pin, called a* mano, *back and forth over the* nixtamal, *grinding the corn into a paste called* masa. *It took about an hour to grind one gallon of* nixtamal *fine enough to make the* masa *used for making tortillas and tamales.*

The second way, they ground dried corn into *very fine cornmeal called* harina de maíz *that was sifted through a horsehair sieve. My great-grandmother (who is 101 years old and lives in Taos) used to grind the corn for her tortillas this way. It is hard, tiring work. Cornmeal mixed with water was used to make tortillas, gorditas (like thick pancakes), and tamales. Today you can buy corn-meal at the supermarket.*

In the old days the women used to make the *tortillas by hand. They would flatten a lump of dough between their palms to make it round and very thin. Now you can make them in a tortilla press. Then you cook them on a* comal, *a flat frying pan without a rim. My father gave my mother a tortilla press for her birthday as a joke, but we buy our tortillas at the supermarket.*

Rosa Gonzales

Here are six ways to eat corn tortillas:

1. Cut them in strips, fry them, and put them in soup.

2. Cut them in strips, fry them, and cook them with tomatoes and chile to make chilaquiles.

3. Fry them and cut them in triangles to make tostadas for dipping in salsa or chile con queso, *which is melted cheese and chile.*

4. Dip them in hot oil, fold them over, and fill them with meat and lettuce and tomatoes and hot sauce to make tacos.

5. Use them to make enchiladas or huevos rancheros.

6. Use them as a scoop for eating beans and other things.

Cornmeal is also used to make tamales. Spicy meat is wrapped in masa. *The meat and dough are then wrapped in cornhusks called* hojas, *which have been soaked all night in a washtub. The tamales are steamed in a big pot. This is what my mother calls labor intensive.*

Two things to remember about tamales:

1. Don't ever eat the hoja. *Once President Gerald Ford tried to eat the cornhusk at a picnic in*

Texas and was very embarrassed when he found out that part isn't eaten.

2. Tamales means more than one. If you eat only one, it's called a tamal, *not a "tamally."*

In Mexico most people eat corn tortillas, but New Mexicans often prefer flour tortillas made from white flour, water, and shortening, rolled out with a rolling pin and baked on a comal. *You eat them plain or make a burrito, a little donkey: wrap a flour tortilla around some kind of filling—meat or beans or scrambled eggs and bacon—and pour red or green chile over the top and sprinkle it with cheese. (My mother says there is too much fat in all of this food, but it is delicious.)*

My father, who is from the Rio Grande Valley in South Texas, told me a story about a poor man who went to work for a rich man. The poor man bragged to the rich man that he was so wealthy he had a different spoon for every meal and never used the same spoon twice. The "spoon" he was talking about was a tortilla.

PETER KINGSTON
AND JOEY BACA

❖

Miracle Dirt

H<small>UDDLED</small> under a tarp in the back of a pickup truck roaring toward Santa Fe, Peter Kingston thought he must have been crazy to tell Joey Baca he'd walk all the way from Santa Fe to Chimayó with him and his family on Good Friday. He peered over at Joey, whose father was driving, and noted with grim satisfaction that he looked cold and sleepy and uncomfortable, too.

It had been a warm spring day when Joey said, "My dad and my grandpa and I are making a pilgrimage to Chimayó on Good Friday. It's about twenty-seven, twenty-eight miles from Santa Fe. Maybe thirty, depending where you start from. It takes the whole day.

You could come with us, if you think you can handle it."

If you think you can handle it! "You're talking about walking?" Peter said scornfully. "That's almost the same as a marathon, you know, and those guys *run* it in a few hours. It's not a race or anything?"

"No, it's a *pilgrimage.* We go to the church, El Santuario de Chimayó. People do it because they made a promise to God or Jesus, not because they want to win or get there first."

"Sure, why not?" Peter said with a shrug, digging into his Frito pie. "Doesn't sound like that big of a deal."

"We'll pick you up at three A.M. Friday," Joey had told him a few days later. "If you still want to do this."

"Three *in the morning?* Are you crazy?"

"It takes at least an hour to drive to Santa Fe," Joey explained patiently. "We start walking about four-thirty. The way my grandfather does it, we average three miles an hour. That works out to nine hours, maybe ten. We get to Chimayó in the afternoon, and my mom picks us up and drives us back. We should be home in time for supper." As an afterthought he had added, "Dress warm."

So there he was, shivering in the back of

the pickup. Joey's mother and father and little sister rode up front in the cab. *The wind-chill factor must be around zero,* Peter thought. And the bed of a truck was a rough ride. It was still too dark to see the mountains.

Peter was a runner. Every day he put on his running shoes and headed up Tramway Boulevard and into the foothills of the Sandías. He loved the quiet up there and the view all the way across the city to the volcanos. Before his parents were divorced, while he and his mother and sister still lived in Los Alamos— "The Hill" they called it—he used to run with his father, a nuclear physicist who had been a champion long-distance runner in college. Now Peter saw his father only every other weekend, so they didn't run together much anymore.

His father expected Peter to be a scientist, too. He encouraged Peter to examine things rationally and think things through logically. "Trust your head," his father lectured him. "Believe what your five senses tell you." There weren't as many of those lectures anymore. He used to hate them; now he kind of missed them.

Peter struggled to find a more comfortable position and bumped into a big wooden beam lying beside him in the bed of the truck. "What's that?" he asked, nudging it with his toe.

"Cross," Joey said. Peter was pleased to see Joey's teeth were chattering.

"What's it for?"

"My dad's going to carry it."

"What's he doing that for?"

"He made a vow."

Peter decided not to ask any more questions. He pulled the tarp up over his face and wished it was all over.

He rememberd when his whole family lived in Los Alamos and his dad sometimes drove them all across the valley to Chimayó, where there was a restaurant they liked a lot. They had never gone to the *santuario,* although they had driven past it, but he remembered the fat sopaipillas, fried dough dripping with honey, and the flan he always had for dessert at the restaurant. The last time he was there was the night his parents took him and Laura out for dinner and calmly announced they were getting a divorce. After that Peter never wanted to go back to the restaurant again.

At around 4:00 A.M., they reached Santa Fe. Mrs. Baca left Joey's sister sleeping with their grandmother and drove the pilgrims to the top of St. Francis Drive. She dropped them off near the Veterans' National Cemetery, where hundreds of plain white crosses were arranged across the hillside in perfect rows. Joey's grandpa picked up a flashlight and a daypack with a Thermos bottle of hot coffee and some cheese sandwiches. Joey and Peter each carried a plastic water bottle. Joey's father eased the heavy wooden cross out of the bed of the pickup and hoisted it onto his shoulder. Mrs. Baca wordlessly hugged each of them, including Peter, and drove off.

They joined a stream of people walking north along the Taos highway. Joey's grandfather walked at the head of their little group, sweeping the ground ahead of them with the beam of his flashlight. Mr. Baca followed him, lugging his cross. Nobody talked much. Peter wished he had worn a woolen hat and turned up the collar of his jacket to cover his ears. It was still the dead of night, and he figured it would start warming up after sunrise.

They moved with maddening slowness. Peter yearned to sprint ahead, run for a couple of miles, and then wait for the rest to catch up. But he kept his pace slow to match theirs.

The highway climbed steeply past the expensive houses on the north side of Santa Fe, still dark and sleeping, and started down the other side. Cars whizzed by them in the darkness.

"Stay off the road," Grandfather warned. He told them about the times people had been hit by cars and killed on the Good Friday pilgrimage.

They passed a mileage sign that said ESPAÑOLA 23 and another one showing the Tesuque turnoff ahead. Next came signs for the Santa Fe Opera. As the inky blackness faded to gray, Peter realized that hundreds of people, maybe thousands, were walking along the highway. Some carried crosses, but most just plodded along with their heads down and their hands shoved deep in their pockets.

"They predicted snow on the TV last night," Grandfather said, studying the overcast sky. "Looks like they were right."

The first flakes began to fall about the time they reached Camel Rock, a pink sandstone formation that really did look like a kneeling camel. A couple of RVs were parked nearby, and a few hardy tourists who had come to look at the rock turned to stare at the pilgrims. One stepped up and snapped a picture of Mr. Baca with his heavy wooden cross.

Peter had ridden up and down this highway a million times without paying attention to the souvenir shops and outlet stores and mobile-home parks. It was as though he was seeing it all for the first time.

"Halfway," Grandfather said when they stopped to use the rest room at a convenience store a couple of miles before the Pojoaque turnoff. "You boys doing all right?"

They nodded. Grandfather looked at Peter's red ears and handed him his cap. "Better put this on," he said. Peter started to object and then accepted the cap gratefully. He really hadn't expected it to be this cold in April. And now the flakes that had been drifting lazily as feathers fell faster, swirling around them and sticking to the pavement. Peter's running shoes were getting wet.

At Pojoaque the highway divided. If you kept going on up the hill, you went through Española and on to Taos; if you took the left lane through the underpass, you were on your way to Los Alamos. Peter wondered how far it was and how long it would take him to walk to The Hill. He could say good-bye to Joey right now and follow the road west toward the Jémez Mountains, past the turnoff to Santa Clara Pueblo, on up the steep, spectacular road to the top of the mesa. Peter could show up at his father's condo and surprise him. But the snowstorm hid everything, and he didn't know how he'd explain that to the Bacas. Or to his father.

They had been walking for more than five hours when they reached the turnoff from the main highway and saw the first road sign for Chimayó. Peter was surprised at how tired he was—this wasn't the same as running. The road narrowed and twisted through orchards of fruit trees with wet, heavy snow clinging to the branches. "This'll kill off all the fruit," Grandfather predicted.

Many more people had joined the pilgrimage along the way. Little kids skipped along beside elderly men and women barely able to hobble. They pulled their coats closer around them, buried their chins in their collars. Cars crawled slowly by them.

For a while Peter walked beside Joey's dad, who stopped frequently to shift the wooden cross from one shoulder to the other. The cross was taller than he was.

"Can I help you carry that?" Peter offered, trying to be polite.

Mr. Baca shook his head and smiled. "It's something I have to do myself," he said. "Thank you."

"Why do you do it?" Peter hoped it wasn't a rude question.

"It's a promise I made. Same as my father made." He nodded at the old man walking ahead of them, talking quietly with Joey. "Pop was in World War II, stationed in the Philippines. He was in the Bataan Death March, and most of his buddies died. He made a vow that if he got back alive, he'd make this pilgrimage every year as long as he was able. He's been doing it for almost fifty years now."

Peter stared admiringly at the old man's straight back. "So how come you do it?" Peter asked again.

"I fought in a different war. Vietnam."

"And you're thankful you survived, right?"

"Yeah. Lost part of a leg, but the rest of me still works pretty good."

Peter didn't say any more. He was aware now of Mr. Baca's limp, which he hadn't noticed before but was becoming more pronounced. Mr. Baca was making this walk with an artificial leg!

They passed through a little settlement with a school and a church. Some of the residents stood shivering by the roadside with coffee and snacks for the pilgrims. Then they were in open country again, the road winding up through the spare, *chamisa*-dotted hills turning white beneath the whirling snow. Crosses stood like lonely sentinels on top of hills too steep for most people to climb.

A sign pointed out the next turnoff: CHI-MAYÓ and SANTUARIO. State policemen in leather jackets directed traffic, trying to keep pedestrians and cars out of each other's way. Knots of people knelt in front of crosses along the sides of the road, and some left a stone at the foot of the cross to show they had stopped there to pray. All Peter could think about was being cold and wet and tired. All he wanted was to get there.

Peter moved with the slow river of people that flowed down the twisting road into the village of Chimayó. They inched painfully through the narrow street and onto the plaza in front of the small adobe church. The plaza was jammed. There was no place to sit and hardly any place to stand, yet more and more pilgrims kept arriving. Some came in wheelchairs. Others struggled with crutches or leaned on canes. A few were crawling on their knees or had taken off their shoes and walked barefoot in the snow. Some looked near exhaustion. Peter reached out to help an old woman who seemed about to faint. Mr. Baca was praying aloud, his limp now so severe that he looked as though he might pitch over.

Besides the religious pilgrims patiently waiting to crowd into the *santuario,* there were also dozens of tourists, toting cameras and milling around as though it was a fiesta of some kind. A television news crew had parked its white van with big blue call letters partly blocking the road, and a news reporter in a bright purple-and-black ski outfit and fuzzy earmuffs was interviewing those who had completed their pilgrimage.

"I'll wait out here," Peter told Joey, who was edging closer to the wide wooden doors. "I could watch your dad's cross for him while he's in there."

"No, no, you have to go inside. Come on. I promised my mother and my grandma I'd take them some dirt."

"Dirt? What dirt?"

But Peter got separated from Joey as the two boys tried to work their way inside the church. Even with all the people crowded into it, the *santuario* was hushed except for the shuffling of feet. Every pew was filled with people kneeling. As some got up, others quickly took their places. At the front of the church, a carved wooden statue of Christ hung above the altar blazing with votive candles. People finished their prayers and waited patiently to pass through a little door near the altar.

"Come on," Joey whispered when he made his way over to Peter.

More candles flickered in a long, narrow room lined with crutches hanging on the walls, colored pictures of saints, snapshots of children and of men in uniform. Peter noticed the statue of a little boy saint inside a glass case with a row of baby shoes lined up at his feet. Joey pulled him on. "In here," he whispered. "This is *El Pozito*."

They squeezed into a tiny room with a doorway so low that most people had to stoop to get through. There were more statues and more candles, but also something else: in the middle of the floor was a hole about six inches wide. A few at a time the pilgrims knelt beside the hole and reached down into it, scooping up handfuls of dirt. Joey pulled a few plastic baggies out of his pocket and handed one to Peter. Peter took it, baffled, but following Joey's example, he scooped a handful of dirt into the baggy.

On the way out Peter saw Joey's father

and grandfather waiting their turn at the hole. Suddenly Peter was starved. His legs ached, his throat felt sore, his head pounded. He felt as though he couldn't breathe, that he was choking on the smell of candles and wet wool.

Then he found himself outside again, gulping lungfuls of cold air. The snow had stopped falling, and sunlight poured through a break in the clouds. People streamed in and out of the souvenir shop nearby, buying religious medals and candles and postcards. Somewhere, Peter hoped, Mrs. Baca was waiting in the pickup to take them back to Santa Fe and then on to Albuquerque. He still clutched the little bag of dirt. "What's this all about?" he asked when he and Joey found a place to sit down for a moment.

"That was *El Pozito*," Joey explained. "It means 'Little Hole.' The dirt in it is holy. It can cure whatever's wrong with you. It works miracles. All those crutches you saw in there? People were cured and left them here."

"I don't believe that," Peter said flatly.

Joey shrugged. "So don't believe it. But it works for some people. My grandma rubs it on her knees where she gets arthritis, and she says it makes her knees stop hurting and she feels better. My mom uses it, too. One time when I fell off my bike and my front teeth went through my lip, my mom put some of the dirt on it and my lip healed right up."

"So you really believe it works?"

"It only works if you believe it's going to work."

Peter was searching for a glimpse of the Bacas' pickup when the women in the fuzzy earmuffs flashed him a big smile and held a microphone like a giant lollipop in front of his mouth.

"What's your name?" she asked brightly. And when he gave it she asked quickly, "Where did you walk from?"

"Santa Fe," he answered. He realized that a TV camera was focused on him.

"And is this your first pilgrimage?"

He licked his lips. "Yes."

"So how do you feel right now?"

"Okay." He tried to back away from the woman and her microphone, but he was trapped—there was no space to move. The amazing thing was that he did feel okay now. A little tired, maybe, but okay.

"Think you'll do it again next year?"

What a dumb question! How did he know what he'd do next year? Then he felt the little bag of dirt in his pocket, and he squeezed it lightly between his fingers. He thought of his father, the Los Alamos physicist, and how his father would laugh about all this, the pilgrimage, *El Pozito,* the little bag of miracle dirt in his pocket. He thought of Mr. Baca, hobbling on his artificial leg, a heavy cross on his shoulder, and of all the people he saw who had struggled to come here. None of them had examined it rationally or thought it through logically. They just believed it.

Who could say then what it was that made Peter answer yes to her dumb question and mean it?

TWO TOWNS:
LOS ALAMOS AND CHIMAYÓ

❧

by Peter Kingston and Joseph Baca

THERE *couldn't be two towns more different from each other than Chimayó and Los Alamos. They are both in northern New Mexico, about thirty miles apart, on opposite sides of the Rio Grande. These towns are famous all over the world, but for totally different reasons.*

Los Alamos is the birthplace of the atomic bomb. Los Alamos means "The Poplars" in Spanish, but long ago it was called by an Indian name that means "Where the Zig-zag Lightning Strikes." In 1942 while our country was at war with Germany and Japan, a group of scientists hunted for a place that was so far away from everything that the world's biggest secret would be safe. The scientists found this high plateau where there wasn't much of anything except a ranch school for rich kids. They sent the students home, and top-secret work began on the Manhattan Project, which was the code name for the research team making the atomic bomb.

Only certain people were allowed to be there. The first scientists who lived at Los Alamos were lucky if they got one of the houses that used to belong to the teachers at the ranch school. This was called Bathtub Row, because they were the only houses that had bathtubs. Otherwise they had to live in flimsy houses without any luxuries. You couldn't leave Los Alamos without filling out a travel form, even if all you wanted to do was go shopping in Santa Fe. You couldn't have your mail sent to Los Alamos. It had to go to a post office box in Santa Fe. Peter Kingston's mother was born in Los Alamos during the war, and it says on her birth certificate that her "place of birth" was Post Office Box 1663, Santa Fe. Her parents weren't even allowed to take a picture of her when she was a baby and send it through the mail. Her mother didn't know what kind of work her husband was doing. Everything was a secret.

The bomb was tested at Trinity Site near White Sands in the southern part of New Mexico on July 16, 1945. It was a success. On August 6, 1945, an atomic bomb was dropped on Hiroshima, Japan. A few days later, another atomic bomb was dropped on Nagasaki. Soon after that the Japanese surrendered, and the war was over.

Los Alamos is an interesting place to live. Peter Kingston, who attended elementary school there, reports that the high-school dropout rate is below one percent. Most kids go to college. The percentage of people with Ph.D. degrees is higher in Los Alamos than anywhere else in the USA.

.   .   .

Chimayó is an entirely different kind of place. It is a small farming community, well known for its weavings and its wood carvings. The name Chimayó comes from an Indian word meaning "obsidian," the name for the black volcanic rock found there.

Chimayó has been a holy place for a long time. The santuario *was built as a private shrine by the Abeyta family and was completed in 1816. Now it belongs to the Catholic Church. There are a lot of stories about the church and about the crucifix that hangs above the altar. There are also legends about the statue of* Santo Niño de Atocha, *the Holy Child who used to roam the countryside at night to help people and always wore out his shoes. Now people leave baby shoes by his statue.*

People say that miracles happen at the santuario *and that the holy dirt from* El Pozito, *The Little Hole, is what cures them.*

Some people call Chimayó the Lourdes of America. (Lourdes is a shrine in France where people go to be cured.) People from all over the world visit the Santuario *year-round, but the week before Easter as many as fifty thousand people come there. Thousands of pilgrims walk to the* santuario *on*

Good Friday. Some of them are hoping for a cure. Others are doing it because they made a promise to God.

Once a group of runners took turns carrying some holy dirt from El Pozito all the way up to Los Alamos. They were praying for peace.

Mr. Alfonso J. Baca, Joseph Baca's grandfather, makes the pilgrimage to Chimayó every year, and he always takes some dirt home to his wife. He believes in milagros—*miracles—but Mrs. Baca says, "It's not the dirt that cures. It's your faith."*

MANUEL MEDINA

✦

Celebration

Manuel Medina watched the party from a quiet corner of the cafetorium, his hands jammed in the pockets of his new pants bought for the occasion. Everybody else was noisily celebrating the publication of *Rio Grande Stories*. His parents were chatting with Teresa Chávez's parents and Ms. Kelsey, who was dressed up in a ruffled red dress. They all seemed to be having a good time, but Manuel was too miserable to join them. He wished he hadn't come at all. And all because he had tried to be the hero in one of his own stories!

The trouble had started because of Manuel's struggles with English. When his family had moved the previous summer from Chihuahua in Mexico, Manuel quickly discovered that learning the new language was harder than he expected. Manuel's father had worked in Albuquerque for several years and could speak English pretty well, but when Manuel and his mother and brothers and sisters arrived, they knew hardly any. For weeks they practiced every evening, watching the news on their small TV because the announcers looked right at you and enunciated each word clearly.

Once a week Manuel's mother took her children to the library, the big one downtown, and checked out armloads of books. Manuel liked the picture books she got for the younger kids because the words were simple and the pictures helped. Manuel dreamed of being a writer. Someday he'd figure out how to write the stories that were always racing around in his head, brave tales of adventure with himself as the dauntless hero. Meanwhile, he read Dr. Seuss to his brothers and sisters.

By the time school started Manuel was doing better with English. He understood much of what was said to him, as long as the speaker didn't rattle it off too fast. His reading skills were really taking off, and his vocabulary was growing by leaps. But he was still having a hard time speaking. The pronunciation rules of English didn't make sense, and he was always mispronouncing things or mixing up words in the wrong order. This was hard. He had been such a good student at his poor school in Mexico, always at the head of his class no matter what it was. Now he felt frustrated and unhappy. As a result, Manuel became self-conscious and shy.

It was his seventh-grade teacher's idea to get him into the Heritage Project. "It will do you a lot of good, Manuel, because you'll be working with other talented students," she promised him. "You're bright, and you'll catch on fast. All you need is a chance to practice." She even went with him for his interview with Mr. Wilder, to give him moral support.

Manuel had been scared to death, but he had managed to tell Mr. Wilder about his great-grandfather who fought with Pancho Villa in the Mexican Revolution, stories he had heard from his father and grandfather. Mr. Wilder didn't seem to mind that he made so many mistakes, and Mr. Wilder's Spanish was good enough to help him out when Manuel got stuck.

"I'm sure you'll add a great deal to the

class, Manuel," Mr. Wilder said, shaking his hand.

"Okay," said Manuel. When he couldn't think of anything else, he said, "Okay."

. . .

Manuel worked hard, although he still had trouble keeping up when the conversation got going too fast and the students all seemed to be talking at once. Most of the kids with Spanish names like Antonio and Rosa didn't help much. They spoke scarcely any Spanish except slang. The exception was Sandra Vargas, who greeted him in Spanish the first day he came to class. But Manuel was too shy to try to talk to her unless she spoke to him first.

Manuel worried endlessly about what he was going to write for the Heritage Project book and how he was going to do it. His written English was still terrible. He could come up with wonderful ideas in his head, all in Spanish, or a mixture of Spanish and English. But when he tried to put the ideas down on paper in English, it was a disaster. He made so many mistakes it sometimes didn't make sense at all, even to him.

Finally, at the start of the spring semester when everyone else seemed to know exactly what they were going to do for the book,

Manuel decided to talk to Mr. Wilder about his problem.

"Why don't you dictate something to one of the other students, Manuel," Mr. Wilder suggested, "or talk into a tape recorder and ask somebody to transcribe it for you? Then you can work together to fix up the grammar and vocabulary. It could be a valuable experience for the coauthor, too."

It had seemed like a good idea, and when Sandra Vargas offered to be his coauthor, Manuel was overjoyed. Besides speaking Spanish, Sandra was nice, and she was also pretty. Her eyes were an amazing green, and her sweet smile lit up her whole face. They had a lot in common, too: she nibbled on her fingernails and so did he.

Manuel intended to tell Sandra some of his family's stories about Pancho Villa. But for some reason on the first day Sandra volunteered to stay after school to begin writing down his story, Manuel launched into a tale, not of Villa's exploits as a kind of Mexican Robin Hood but of how he, Manuel Medina, had crossed the Rio Grande from Mexico and sneaked into the United States, right under the nose of *la migra,* the Border Patrol.

The more Manuel talked, the bigger

Sandra's eyes grew. He kept adding more and more to his story, making it sound as though he had done something very scary and dangerous: wading across the river at night, his clothes tied up in a bundle; hiding in the brush while *la migra,* alerted by sensors that someone had just crossed the river, roared by in their van, shining their bright lights in every direction; being caught and forced into the back of the van to ride around for hours while the Immigration and Naturalization Service agents picked up other "wets," the insulting word they use for the immigrants; and then being driven to the bridge and sent back across to Mexico.

"I did it two more times, sneaked across the river at two other places," Manuel said while Sandra scribbled furiously to keep up with him.

The third time, according to this tale he was spinning as he went along, he managed to make his way north to Albuquerque, almost dying of thirst because he didn't have any water with him as he crossed *la Jornada del Muerto,* the Journey of Death, the desert in the southern part of New Mexico.

Manuel's invented story was patched together from real accounts he had heard from other people, from friends of his parents, but he pretended all this had happened to him. Although his parents were Mexican, they had "green cards"—documents making them legal residents. He had actually come to Albuquerque on a bus. It hadn't been dangerous at all.

Not long after he had made up this tale for her, Sandra had brought him his story, carefully typed in perfect English. Naturally he was too ashamed to admit then that none of his tale of adventure was true. He couldn't bring himself to look in her beautiful green eyes. When Mr. Wilder asked how he was doing with his story for the book, Manuel shrugged and said, "I have to think about it some more."

The next time Sandra asked him about it, he looked away and told her he had changed his mind. He didn't want to have his story printed in the book, he said. "I could get somebody in trouble with it."

"What about Pancho Villa?" Sandra asked him. "We could still do that story, you know. If you want to."

But Manuel just shook his head. He felt guilty and foolish. It had been a stupid thing to do, and he wished he could unsay every word. After a while Sandra stopped asking him, until finally it was too late to write anything at all for the book.

Instead, Manuel decided to work hard to raise money for *Rio Grande Stories,* even if he didn't have a story in it. Teresa Chávez, the business manager, organized a group to get advance sales. They were to talk as many people as possible (mostly their parents and other relatives) into paying in advance for the book, fifty cents less than the price of the book after it was published, so they'd have enough money to cover printing and binding costs. Manuel visited the manager of the coffee shop on the corner of his block and convinced her to take a half dozen copies at the special price to sell at the cash register along with the Spanish-language newspaper.

When Sara McGinley and Rebecca Rivera made up fliers advertising the book, Manuel took a stack around to other schools and to the public library and posted them on the bulletin boards. He stapled them on utility poles near the university alongside advertisements for poetry readings and jazz concerts.

The day the first copies of *Rio Grande Stories* came back from the printer everyone in the Heritage Project had excitedly flipped through the pages bound with plastic spirals and bright turquoise covers. The book was really handsome. Manuel wished more than ever that he had a story in it.

Having the party was Ms. Kelsey's idea. "You've done something to be proud of, students," she said. "Certainly a celebration is in order." By the next day plans were already in the works. Parents agreed to bring donations of food for snacks, and the principal, Mrs. Salazar, arranged for the paper napkins and cups and plates. Manuel volunteered to help.

On the day of the party Franklyn and Jacquelyn Cox brought balloons and paper streamers and Manuel stayed after school with them to blow up the balloons and drape the streamers—turquoise, like the cover of the book—around the cafetorium. Sara McGinley and her parents arrived to set up dozens of luminarias to show the way. Manuel helped, filling dozens of paper bags with sand.

Finally, on the way home, he stopped at a florist and bought his mother a corsage with his lunch money.

But now, on the night of the party celebrating the publication of *Rio Grande Stories,* he felt terrible. In spite of all his hard work, his conscience still bothered him. Manuel slouched in a corner of the cafetorium, feeling worse than he had ever felt in his life, watching everyone else have a good time.

It was Mr. Wilder's suggestion that each student invite somebody who was important to that person's heritage. Ricky Begay brought his grandfather, dressed in his special code talker uniform from World War II, plus some beautiful silver-and-turquoise bracelets and necklaces. Tony Martínez showed up with a guy dressed like a priest in a long black cassock and white collar, and introduced him to everybody as Padre Martínez of Taos. He turned out really to be an actor who played the role of the priest who Tony was still insisting could have been his great-great-great-something-grandfather.

Manuel's parents had come, his mother wearing the pretty yellow flowers he had bought her, but he couldn't think of anyone else to invite. If he could have gotten out of it, he wouldn't have brought his mother and father either, but he knew they'd have been disappointed. They'd be even more disappointed if they knew why he didn't have a story in the book.

"I asked my *primo* if he'd drive down in

his low rider for the party," Tomás Jaramillo told Manuel, "but he can't."

"Don't be too disappointed," Sara Mc-Ginley said. "I wanted to bring my burro, but they wouldn't let me."

Manuel wasn't a bit surprised when Jacquelyn Cox swept in wearing a prim black suit and a black hat over a white scarf. "Since I can't *bring* Georgia O'Keeffe," Jacquie announced dramatically, "I shall *be* Georgia O'Keeffe." That was Jacquie's style. She was always appearing at school in some outlandish costume, announcing that she was an African queen or some figure from history.

Franklyn Cox was nothing like his sister. He stayed with his parents—his father in his Air Force dress blues—and an aged black man with a cane whom he introduced simply as "my friend Steven."

Ricky Begay had brought his camera and started snapping pictures—"Georgia O'Keeffe," of course, and then Jeremy Steinberg, all dressed up in a suit and tie, and Rosa holding copies of the book. "Come on, Manuel," Ricky said. "You get in the picture, too." But Manuel refused. He didn't deserve to be in the photograph.

Instead he sidled over to the food table and pretended to look at the wonderful things people had brought. In the place of honor was a giant cake decorated with a cartoon drawing in colored icing of a low rider. Scrolled across the top of the cake was the message:

CONGRATULATIONS HERITAGE PROJECT KIDS

and below the car was written:

Rio Grande Stories

with the first names of all the students in the class arranged around the car. Ricky was busy making a portrait of it.

While Manuel watched Ricky fool with his camera, Jeremy came by and helped himself to a couple of *bizcochitos*. Besides his parents he had brought his grandfather and a tiny white-haired lady in a wheelchair.

"What a beautiful cake," the lady said.

"As soon as Ricky takes the picture," Jeremy said, "I think we should cut it."

"Oh, not yet!" said Rosa Gonzales, who had led her mother over to see it. "It seems like a shame to eat it."

"Why not? That's what it's for, isn't it?"

Manuel almost smiled. Jeremy and Rosa

had been arguing for months. But they seemed to like each other after all.

Jeremy was reaching for the cake knife when there was a flurry of activity at the door and somebody shouted, "The TV people are here!"

"TV people?"

"I think your father decided to come to the party, Rosa," said Ms. Kelsey excitedly, rushing over in a flutter of red ruffles.

Rosa gasped, and Manuel recognized Andy Gonzales, anchor for the evening news, flashing his familiar grin and followed by a cameraman and a couple of other people lugging TV equipment. This was the man with the clear enunciation who had helped him learn English. The teachers and parents hung back, but the other kids crowded around—all but Manuel.

While the crew set up lights at the table where *Rio Grande Stories* was displayed, Rosa led her father over to Jeremy Steinberg. A minute later Andy Gonzales held a microphone in front of Jeremy and asked him about the book.

"We wanted to help raise money for a sculpture for the school," Jeremy explained. "It was our idea to do a book about our cultural heritage. We've been working on it since last fall." Jeremy picked up a copy of the book and held it up for the camera. "These stories represent a cross section of the cultures in our Heritage Project class. Lots of people worked on it," he said, "but Rosa Gonzales is the one who brought it all together."

Rosa's father turned to her and held the mike in front of her. "Tell us about some of the stories, Ms. Gonzales."

For the next minute or so Rosa described the articles in the book—Pauline's about Indian pots, Franklyn's about Estebanico, April's about chile.

"And yours, Ms. Gonzales?"

"I wrote about tortillas!" she said proudly.

Manuel envied how easily both Jeremy and Rosa spoke in front of a camera, as though they had spent their lives doing interviews. He would have been petrified.

Within minutes the crew had packed up all their equipment, Mr. Gonzales had shaken hands with a few of the parents, waved to the cheering kids, and was on his way out the door. "Be sure to watch the ten o'clock news!" he called and was gone.

When the excitement had died down, Mrs.

Salazar climbed up on the stage and made a little speech, thanking everyone for coming, for bringing the wonderful food, and so on. She explained to the parents and guests that all of the profits from the sale of books would go toward buying the sculpture. "A famous artist has agreed to make it," she told them. "This artwork is going to make Rio Grande Middle School famous. The theme of the sculpture, which will have water flowing through it, is the river and how it connects people through time and across cultures. The name of the sculpture, of course, is *Río Grande*."

Applause, murmurs of approval, and pleased surprise greeted her announcement.

Then Mrs. Salazar introduced Mr. Wilder, and the kids cheered again, and when Ms. Kelsey was introduced and got up on the stage and gave her little wave, there were whistles and applause mixed in with the cheers. Manuel glanced at Teresa Chávez, who was grinning and clapping madly. Mr. Wilder introduced Jeremy and Rosa, the editors, and Teresa, the business manager.

Then the worst thing imaginable happened: Teresa called on the director of sales,

Manuel Medina, to come up on the stage and say a few words about all the money they were making.

Manuel was in a panic. If there was one thing he couldn't do, it was get up and talk in front of people. That was even worse than attempting to write something! But he knew he had to try. A thin glaze of sweat formed on his forehead. Manuel saw his parents beaming proudly up at him and took a deep breath. He would show them that he did have some courage after all.

"We have sold one hundred fifty copies in advance," he reported. "Our goal is to sell five hundred copies. That will give us a profit of five hundred dollars."

Everyone clapped again, and Manuel stepped down. He had said only a few words, but he had done it, and he felt that he had behaved bravely, as his parents would expect. If only he could forget for a few hours the lies he had told Sandra, it would be a happy evening for him, too. But he couldn't, and it wasn't.

People were starting to drift away and Jeremy and Manuel began to pack up the unsold books. Manuel had counted the money taken in that evening, almost a hundred dollars.

Good, he thought, *but not good enough.* They would have to work hard to sell out all of these.

"Don't worry," said Rosa, coming over to help them. "We're going to sell them all. You'll see. We might even have to print up more."

At that moment Tomás Jaramillo tore into the cafetorium shouting, "He's here! He's here!"

"Who's he talking about?" Jeremy asked.

"His low-rider cousin, I'll bet!" Rosa said. "Maybe he's brought his car."

It was Tomás's cousin, all right, but Johnny Aragón hadn't brought his magnificent car. What he brought instead was an idea. Tomás jumped up on the stage and waved his arms until he got everyone's attention.

"He's going to bring the car down next Saturday, and we can park it at Coronado Mall and sell our books out of the trunk," he said proudly. "I know we'll sell a lot of them, too, because *Mi Güisa*'s going to attract a whole lot of attention."

Despite all this good news, Manuel still felt bad. He looked around for his parents. Instead he saw Sandra, whom he had been avoiding all evening, coming toward him.

"That was really good, Manuel," Sandra said, stepping close and lightly touching his arm. "I bet you'll do just great when you present all the money to Mrs. Salazar at the school assembly next month."

He thought for a minute he was going to be sick. "I have to do that?"

"Don't worry," she said, concern creasing her face. "Are you okay? You look kind of funny."

"I lied," Manuel said in a choking voice.

"What?"

"I lied. About crossing the border. It wasn't like that at all. I came on a bus. I'm sorry." He felt like crying.

She smiled a smile like sunshine. "Oh that! It doesn't matter, Manuel. I thought you were kind of stretching things. Did you have any cake yet?"

She knew all along! Manuel sighed and wiped his face with the handkerchief his mother had given him. Never again would he tell a lie, he promised himself as he let Sandra lead him to the table where the cake was rapidly disappearing. He found the piece with part of his name on it: *anuel*. Somebody had eaten the *M*.

And then it was time to leave. "You'll all

want to be home in time to watch the late news!" Mrs. Salazar reminded them. Manuel had promised to stay and clean up after the guests had gone, but that didn't take long because a few others—Sandra Vargas among them—also stayed to help. A handful of parents were waiting, including Mr. and Mrs. Medina. Manuel's mother hugged him, and his father thumped him on the back.

As the lights in the school blinked out, Manuel and his parents walked past the spot where *Río Grande* would soon stand.

HOW TO PRONOUNCE
NAMES AND PLACES

❖

Abeyta (*ah-BAY-tah*)

Abiquiú (*ah-bee-KYOO*)

Aguas Calientes (*AH-gwahss cah-lee-EHN-tayss*)

Albuquerque (*AHL-buh-ker-kee*)

Antonio (*ahn-TOH-nyoh*)

Aragón (*ah-rah-GOHN*)

Arturo (*ar-TOO-roh*)

Cabeza de Vaca (*kah-BAY-sah deh BAH-kah; deh VAH-kah*)

Carlota (*kar-LOH-tah*)

Catalina (*kah-tah-LEE-nah*)

Chama (*CHAH-mah*)

Chávez (*CHAH-vess*)

Chihuahua (chee-WAH-wah)

Chimayó (*chee-my-OH*)

Cíbola (*SEE-boh-lah*)

Cochití (*koh-chee-TEE*)

Consuelo (*kohn-SWAY-loh*)

Cortés, Hernán (*kor-TESS, ehr-NAHN*)

Dineh (*dee-NEH*)

Dorantes (*doh-RAHN-tayss*)

Durango (*doo-RAHN-goh*)

Eduardo (*ed-WAR-doh*)

Enrique (*en-REE-kay*)

Española (*ess-pah-NYOH-lah*)

Estebanico (*ess-tay-bahn-EE-koh*)

Flores (*FLOH-rayss*)

García (*gar-SEE-ah*)

Gonzales (*gon-SAH-layss*)

Gregorio (*greh-GOHR-yo*)

Guadalupe (*gwah-dah-LOO-pay*)

Jaramillo (*hah-rah-MEE-yo*)

Jémez (*HAY-mess*)

Jornada del Muerto (*hohr-NAH-dah del MWEHR-toh*)

José (*hoh-SAY*)

Juárez (*HWAH-ress*)

Llorona (*yoh-ROH-nah*)

Los Alamos (*lohss AH-la-mohss*)

Malinche (*mah-LEEN-chay*)

Manuel (*mahn-WEL*)

Martínez (*mahr-TEE-ness*)

Medina (*meh-DEE-nah*)

Mondragón (*mohn-drah-GOHN*)

Nuevomexicanos (*NWAY-voh-meh-hee-KAH-nos*)

Ortega (*or-TAY-gah*)

Pizarro (*pee-SAH-ro*)

Pojoaque (*poh-HWAH-kay*)

Reyes (*RAY-ayss*)

Río Abajo (*REE-oh ah-BAH-ho*)

Río Arriba (*REE-oh ah-REE-bah*)

Río Grande (*REE-oh GRAHN-day*)

Rivera (*ree-VEH-rah*)

Salazar (*sah-lah-SAHR*)

San Felipe de Neri (*sahn feh-LEE-pay deh NEH-ree*)

Sánchez (*SAHN-chess*)

Sandías (*sahn-DEE-ahs*)

Sangre de Cristo (*SAHN-gray deh KREE-stoh*)

Santa Cruz (*SAHN-tah KROOS*)

Santa Fe (*SAHN-tah FAY*)

Santo Niño de Atocha (*SAHN-toh NEE-nyoh deh
ah-TOH-chah*)

Taos (*TOWSS*)

Teresa (*teh-RAY-sah*)

Tesuque (*teh-SOO-kay*)

Tewa (*TEH-wah*)

Tierra Amarilla (*TYEH-rah ah-ma-REE-yah*)

Tomás (*toh-MAHSS*)

Torquemada (*tor-keh-MAH-thah*)

Vargas (*VAHR-gahss*)

Zuni (*ZOO-nee*)

HOW TO PRONOUNCE
SOME COMMON WORDS—
AND WHAT THEY MEAN

abuela (*ah-BWAY-lah*) — grandmother

acequia (*ah-SEH-kyah*) — ditch

bizcochito (*BEES-koh-CHEE-toh*) — cookie

bosque (*BOHS-kay*) — woods

bruja (*BROO-hah*) — witch

burrito (*boo-REE-toh*) — literally, little
donkey; filled
tortilla

burro (*BOO-roh*) — donkey

cabrito (*kah-BREE-toh*) — young goat

calabacitas (*kah-lah-bah-SEE-tahs*) — squash and
chile

calabaza (*kah-lah-BAH-sah*) — squash

camposanto (*kahm-poh-SAHN-toh*) — cemetery

chamisa (*chah-MEE-sah*) — sagebrush

chicharrones (*chee-chah-RHO-nayss*) — fried pork
skins

chilaquiles (*chee-lah-KEE-layss*) — dish made
with tortillas

chile con queso (*CHEE-leh kohn KAY-soh*) —
chile with cheese

chile relleno (*CHEE-leh ray-YAY-noh*) —
stuffed chile

cholo (*CHO-loh*) — punk, dude

chongo (*CHOHN-goh*) — Navajo ponytail

comal (*koh-MAHL*) — iron griddle

conquistadores (*kohn-kee-stah-DOH-rehs*) —
conquerors

curandera (*koo-ran-DEH-rah*) — healer

diablo (*DYAH-bloh*) — devil

don (*DOHN*) — gift, talent

enchilada (*ehn-chee-LAH-dah*) — dish made with
tortillas

enjarradora (*ehn-hahr-rah-DOH-rah*) — woman
who
plasters

enjarrar (*ehn-hahr-RAHR*) — to plaster

Feliz Navidad (*feh-LEESS nah-vee-DAHD*) —
Merry Christmas

flan (*FLAHN*) — caramel custard

gordita (*gohr-DEE-tah*) — cornmeal pancake

gringa (*GREEN-gah*) — English-speaking white
woman

güisa (*HWEE-sah*) — sweetheart

hacienda (*ah-SYEHN-dah*) — ranch house

harina de maíz (*ah-REE-nah deh mah-EESS*) —
fine cornmeal

hijita (*ee-HEE-tah*) — little daughter

hoja (*OH-hah*) — corn shuck for tamales

horno (*OR-noh*) — outdoor oven

huevos rancheros (*WEH-vohs rahn-CHEH-rohs*) — eggs with beans and chile

kiva (*KEE-vah*) — Pueblo Indian place of
worship

latilla (*lah-TEE-yah*) — wood lath

llano (*YAH-noh*) — plain

luminaria (*loo-mee-NAHR-yah*) — paper lantern

maíz (*mah-EESS*) — maize; corn

mal ojo (*mahl OH-ho*) — evil eye

mano (*MAH-noh*) — stone roller

masa (*MAH-sah*) — corn meal dough

metate (*meh-TAH-teh*) — stone for grinding corn

migra (*MEE-grah*) — immigration official

milagro (*mee-LAH-groh*) — miracle

muchas gracias (*MOO-chas GRAH-syahs*) — many thanks

nacimiento (*nah-see-MYEHN-toh*) — manger; crèche

naja (*NAH-hah*) — part of necklace

natillas (*nah-TEE-yahss*) — boiled custard

nixtamal (*neesh-tah-MAHL*) — ground corn

padre (*PAH-dray*) — father

pesos (*PEH-sohss*) — Mexican currency

piloncillo (*pee-lohn-SEE-yoh*) — raw sugar

piñon (pee-NYOHN) — pine

por favor (*pohr-fah-VOHR*) — please

posadas (*poh-SAH-dahss*) — inns

posole (*poh-SOH-leh*) — hominy stew

pozito (*poh-SEE-toh*) — little hole

primo (*PREE-moh*) — cousin

pueblo (*PWEH-bloh*) — town

quinceañera (*keen-seh-ah-NYEH-rah*) —
fifteenth birthday celebration

remedios (*reh-MEH-dyohss*) — remedies

ristra (*REE-strah*) — string of chiles

santero (*sahn-TEH-roh*) — carver of wooden
saints

santuario (*sahn-TWAH-ryoh*) — sanctuary;
church

sopaipilla (*soh-pah-PEE-yah*) — fried bread

tamal; tamales (*tah-MAHL; tah-MAH-layss*) —
meat with cornmeal and chile

tía (*TEE-yah*) — aunt

tortilla (*tor-TEE-yah*) — thin corn cake

tostadas (*tohs-TAH-dahss*) — tortilla chips

viga (*VEE-gah*) — roof beam

P.S. Spanish is often written with accent marks above certain vowels. The marks indicate which syllable is stressed if it is different from the way the word would be pronounced under the usual (but complicated, if you don't speak Spanish) rules.